I0666902

HEARTBEAT

A Lovers' Heart Series, Book Two

CHERYL BARTON

Published by: Cheryl Barton Publishing, LLC

This book is a work of fiction and any references or similarities to actual events, real people, living or dead, or to real places, are intended to give the novel a sense of reality. Any similarities in names, characters, places and incidents is entirely coincidental.

For permission requests, write to the publisher, addressed "Attention: Permissions Coordinator," at the address below.

Cheryl Barton Publishing, LLC
P.O. Box 962
Reisterstown, Maryland 21136
www.crbarton.com

Ordering Information:
Quantity sales. Special discounts are available on quantity purchases by corporations, associations, and others. For details, contact the publisher at the address above.

Orders by U.S. trade bookstores and wholesalers. Please contact prez@crbarton.com

ISBN-13: 978-1978950-02-2
ISBN:1-948950-02-2

Dear Reader,

Well, here we are with the next installment of *A Lovers' Heart* book series, *Heartbeat*.

In book one, *Heartthrob*, there was Cade Weston's story where he proved that playboys need love, too. Now, it's time to enjoy his brother, Navy SEAL Calvin Lymon's story, a man so focused on work that he wasn't prepared for love hitting him, not once, but twice.

Calvin's story was special to me because oftentimes, fathers get the short end of the stick when it comes to caring for and loving their children. Here you have a man whose first priority is protecting his son from a menace while allowing his heart to fall in love once again.

Find that quiet spot, grab your cup of tea and indulge in Calvin's story. You won't be able to avoid falling in love with his love!

Happy Reading!

Cheryl Barton

ABOUT HEARTBEAT

In book two of, "A Lovers' Heart" series, Navy SEAL, Calvin Lymon, was about his country's business when he allowed himself to cross the line and his heart got involved resulting in a love lost. Injured in the line of duty, he fights to stay alive for the sake of his newborn son, Camico.

A new city and a new outlook on life were exactly what physical therapist, Ava Cortez, needed after years of living life alone and off the grid to avoid being detected by a madman. She never allowed herself to love anyone, especially a man, afraid she would be found out. When she's asked to oversee the therapy of a sexy navy SEAL, she tries to fight the immediate and intoxicating lure to a man who exudes more sexual potency than she's ever experienced. Can she forget about business and indulge in pleasure for once?

Calvin deals with the days of therapy that drain him, but nothing compares to the salacious, steamy nights of passion with Ava that are having the biggest impact on his ability to get back to reality until an old rival resurfaces and threatens his life and his loves.

Once and for all, Calvin knows he has to deal with his past and risk losing his woman and his son, who are his heartbeats.

<u>Bachelor Series</u>

Bachelor Not for Sale
A Designed Affair
A Perfect Combination
Love at Last
Twelve Bachelors for Sale – Coming 2018

<u>Amorous Occupations Series</u>

The Artist
The Bookkeeper
The Chef
The Dancer
The Electrician

<u>A Lovers' Heart Series</u>

Heartthrob
Heartbeat
Heartbreaker – Coming 2018

<u>Stand Alone Romance Novels</u>

Holly for Christmas
Snowbound
Cupid's Arrow
One Wish
His Halloween Promise
Home for Thanksgiving
Holly for Christmas
A Better Man
Bossy
Un-Break My Heart
Love on Top
Take a Knee
Love at First Sight
My First Love
Black Love

PROLOGUE

Cade's cell phone rang.

"Damn," he bellowed. "I thought I turned that off. Let me do it now before it rings again."

Cade reached for it and glanced at who would call him at this late hour. His body stiffened when a text message appeared on the screen and he saw the code that appeared. It was a code that he and his younger brothers, Cameron and Calvin had created that meant that there was an emergency. The first four digits of the code were the same for all of them, but when it was followed by the number eight, he knew the emergency was Calvin. Something was wrong.

In bed with his wife, Callie, Cade sat up quickly and dialed the satellite phone that he'd provided for both of his brothers to reach him at all times, no matter where any of them were in the world.

"Cade, what's wrong?" Callie asked, frightened when she saw the grave look on his face.

"I don't know, baby. It's Calvin and something's wrong. He sent me a text to call with the emergency code and the number he called me from was his satellite phone. We only use those in case of an emergency and after all of these years, this is the first time he's used it."

Callie got right up, grabbed her gown, pulling it over her head before coming around to his side of the bed. She sat next to him as he completed dialing the number.

"Calvin?" he asked when the line picked up.

"No, it's not Calvin, this is Mason one of Calvin's friends. There's been an accident and Calvin's been injured. I'm not supposed to call you because we were on a secret mission, but Calvin gave me this information to reach out to you if anything ever happened to him."

Cade's heart stopped beating as he waited for more information. He never thought he'd get the dreaded call that something had happened to Calvin who was a navy SEAL. He knew his brother went on dangerous missions and always prayed for his safety.

"How bad is he?" he asked.

"He's pretty bad. The military is flying him back to the states for medical care, but I want to warn you, his injuries are pretty severe."

"Tell me where they're sending him and I'll meet the carrier," Cade said anxiously.

"That's not a problem, but that's not the only reason I'm calling you."

"There's more?" he asked, anxiously.

"Let me explain as much as I can, but then I'll need to hang up. I'm not supposed to tell you this. Calvin was in the middle of a mission to rescue a woman from her family and take down her father and brother who are powerful in the drug and gun-running business. During the mission, he was injured, the woman was killed and so was her brother and his men. Her father survived and has gone into hiding. The woman's child survived and no one knows about the baby except me. Some of his mother's friends are looking after him, but I need to get him out of Colombia and on American soil."

There was a pause and Cade was losing patience to hear more. Why was he being told about some woman's child when his brother was injured, perhaps severely.

"What are you not telling me Mason?" he asked nervously.

"The baby is Calvin's son, Cade. The woman and Calvin had been seeing each other secretly for some time."

Cade stiffened.

"A baby? Calvin has a baby and the mother was killed?" he asked, shocked.

Callie heard it all, got up and began packing a bag for Cade knowing that as soon as he got off of the phone, he would be leaving. She picked up the house phone and called Aaron, Cade's head of security, on his cell.

"Aaron, Cade is going to need the jet tonight. I don't have the destination yet, but he has a family emergency. As soon as I have where he needs to go so that the pilot can file a flight plan, I'll call you back, but in the meantime, can you get the pilot up and to the airport? He should be ready to take off as soon as Cade gets there. He needs you and Sean here immediately."

She hung just as Cade disconnected his call.

"I'm packing you a bag and Aaron is getting your plane ready. What else happened?" she said rushing about the room.

Cade got up and started dressing in the clothes she'd laid out.

"The short story is Calvin was injured on a mission while rescuing a woman and taking down her family. This is some woman he'd been having a secret affair with. During the mission, she was killed, but the baby survived. He's a little boy named Camico and Mason, the guy who called, is getting the baby safely to this country. He's texting me the information on where they are sending Calvin. I'm going to finish dressing. Check my phone and when he texts the information, call Aaron and give it to him, so he'll know where we're going. I need to get to the hospital when they bring Calvin in."

"What about the baby?" she asked.

Cade stopped in his tracks. He has a nephew who was alone and he needed to get him.

"Mason said it would be a day before the baby gets to the states. I don't know what to do about him yet. I have to think it through. It's a baby and he's family. I need to get to him and get to Calvin."

Callie knew what to do.

"When the baby arrives in the states, send the jet to pick him up and bring him to Texas to the ranch. See if Abby can help with getting him to me and I'll look after him while you look after your brother."

"You're the best, baby. Call Cam for me and get him moving. Tell him we have a family emergency and Calvin needs us. He needs both of his brothers by his side."

CHAPTER ONE

Navy SEAL, Calvin Lymon's body purred to life with a desirous hunger unlike anything he had ever experienced before. The word, stunning, streaked like lightning across his mind the moment the statuesque beauty came into his line of sight in the overcrowded pub in the heart of Colombia, South America. The essence of her tantalizing aura radiated so far out from her actual body that everything about her engulfed his very being like a tight embrace that covered him completely.

Calvin couldn't take his eyes away even if he wanted to. Even though the room was packed with patrons from one dusty beige wall to the next, from across the room and through every person that covered the path between them, the woman of his admiring gaze stood out. He watched every scrupulously slow move as she danced and swayed to the Latin music playing loudly through speakers that were placed in all four corners of the large, spacious room.

A lump formed in his throat causing him to gulp in disbelief at the immediate impact her loveliness had on him. He had seen and indulged in his share of beautiful women before, but none compared to the woman his eyes were locked on.

Slowly changing the direction of his stare, he looked downward toward the gray and black marbled tiled floor where she stood and his eyes covered her from her brightly painted red toe nails that peaked out at him through strappy white high-heeled stilettos and up her long-toned chestnut brown legs which were visible because of the short white body hugging dress she had on.

From there, he let his eyes continue on their path to hips that flared out, just below her slim waste showcasing her hourglass figure. The way she moved had his mind traveling to a place in time where he imagined himself holding on to all of her curves tightly as her legs wrapped snugly around his hips allowing his body to sink into hers in the most intimate and provocative way. He shifted in his seat as his manhood jumped when his eyes continued an upward path landing on her full, large breasts, the part of a woman that he admired first when it came to the physicality of a sexy woman. His mouth felt as dry as the Mohave desert with a tongue that was as heavy as lead as lascivious thoughts around all he could do with a body like hers flooded through him.

Anxiety overtook him when those in the crowd

walking by blocked his view of her as if the very life was being sucked from his body. A sheer moment of disconnect had his heart racing while he stretched his neck as if keeping his eyes on her was what kept his heart beating, giving him life.

Finding an opening, again, the beauty once again came into focus and this time, as she danced, she turned around and he finally got the chance to see her face. To say she was beautiful didn't quite capture the full, powerful punch of her exquisiteness. He had never seen a more perfect woman in his entire life and he had a feeling, he probably never would again. He couldn't focus on anything else other than his life depending on him getting his fill of looking at her.

Her long dark hair flowed down around her shoulders moving in sync with her body's movements. When she raised her hands above her head and slowly swayed down toward the floor, Calvin almost fell off of the chair he'd been sitting on, snapping him briefly out of the trance the beauty had him in.

Remembering to breathe, he looked around and checked to see if anyone else saw what he did and by the look on every guy's face in the pub, he wasn't the only one who noticed her; he wasn't surprised.

A feeling of possession overcame him as he turned his face up in a sneer at every man who looked at her the way he was looking at her. He wanted her, yes, and he assumed every man in the place did as well and he didn't like it one bit. Little did they know that he was Calvin Lymon, Navy SEAL and he had enough confidence to overshadow everyone in the room. This woman was his and there was no way he would lose out on an opportunity to meet her nor would he watch another man spend the night getting to know her the way he was planning to do. No one knew, but she was meant for him.

"You okay, Cal?"

Somewhere in what seemed like a distant place, Calvin heard someone addressing him as Cal, what family and close friends called him, but he couldn't focus on the words because he didn't want to take his attention away from the woman of his dreams. The voice had to be that of Mason, his best friend and fellow Navy SEAL. No one else from their team had accompanied them on their one day off from surveillance in the foreign country. He tried his best to tamper down the intrusion of Mason's voice because it was distracting.

Turning back to the woman who had already stolen his heart, he watched as she moved left and then right until she was again standing tall. The moment she threw her head back and laughed at something, what he didn't know, his libido went off the charts like never before. His body hardened like impenetrable steel.

"Cal, can you hear me?"

He heard the voice again, but didn't want to

focus on it just in case the woman in front of him wasn't real, but possibly a mirage. Can any woman really be that beautiful? She was perfection and she would be what a man would call a total package. Everything about her was flawless and the way she carried herself, her magnetism wasn't just externally, but he sensed a strong, confident woman internally, something that meant more to him than what he could see with his eyes.

"Cal? Give me a sign that you hear me?"

Now annoyed that he was being interrupted, he huffed out a response.

"Yes, I can hear you," he said in his head because his mouth wouldn't move. What was wrong with his mouth? He tried again to form words to actually speak, but nothing came out. He could only hear his answer in his head, perhaps due to the loud music wafting out from the speakers.

In an instant, for some reason, the crowd milled back into focus right in front of him, thereby blocking his view of her. He slid down from the stool and tried to find her again as his heart beat sped up and uneasiness put his nerves on edge at the thought that he may have lost his chance because he allowed himself to be distracted by a voice. He didn't want to lose sight of her because he needed to meet her. He needed to tell her that though he'd only set eyes on her for a few minutes, he never wanted to live another day without seeing her beautiful face over and over again.

Calvin wasn't sure he'd actually been living until the moment he'd spotted her. Now, the word, complete, came to mind because that would be the state of his love life if he were able to convince her that they were meant for each other.

"What are you thinking about, Cal?" he heard as he started making his way through the throngs of people who gathered and were now in his way.

Calvin knew he was thinking one thing and one thing only and that was to get to this woman and start a connection he hoped would lead to him showing her that he could be the man of her dreams.

As he pushed his way forward, the crowd seemed to thicken even more as he forced his way through to her. He could hear voices calling out to him and though he wasn't focusing on them, they were familiar. Dismissing them, he didn't want to talk to anyone other than the woman who was the focus of his full attention.

Coming to the point where he thought she had been standing, he couldn't spot her anywhere. Anxiously, he looked around as his heart began to pound in his chest with the thought that she had indeed left and he would never get the chance to talk to her, to get to know her or to let her know that she had such an immediate impact on him that his life would be nothing if he didn't have her in it.

Not seeing her anywhere, he held his head in disappointment as he turned and made his way back toward his seat at the bar. Coming through the crowd, he walked up to the stool, turned and when he looked up, there she was right in front of him and smiling. When she wiggled her finger at him to come closer, he pointed to himself to be sure she was talking to him. When she nodded yes, he was ecstatic with delight thinking that she must have been watching him as he was watching her and maybe even feeling the connection he'd felt.

As if from a scene in a movie, the crowd parted, clearing a path straight to her. As he began to move in her direction, the smile on her face turned into a frightening frown, one laced with fear and overwrought with terror. He watched as her hand reached up to the side of her neck covering it as her eyes beamed with dread. Looking from her face to where her hand landed, he could see bright red blood begin to seep through her fingers, covering her hand and sliding down to stain the white dress she was wearing. He looked on in horror as she then reached to her stomach where another big red patch of blood began to form and coat the fingers of her other hand. What was happening, he thought as he felt helpless at coming to her aid?

Without thinking, Calvin began running to her, reaching her at the moment when she collapsed to the floor. Holding her in his arms, he could hear her plead with him to help her. He looked around and was stunned to see people were still dancing as if the most beautiful girl in the world was not bleeding to death on the floor right in front of them. He looked for Mason and called out to him for help, but the music was so loud, he knew Mason wouldn't be able to hear him.

Calvin tried to lift her up to get her to a hospital, but her body felt like lead. As her eyes began to close and her hands dropped away, Calvin was puzzled as to what happened. Had she been stabbed? Was it a shooter? He looked around for anything and saw nothing, but crowds of people dancing to the music, laughing and drinking. He tried putting pressure on her neck and then on her side and screamed for anyone to help him. He reached for the person closest to him, but he couldn't get a good grip on his pant leg. His hand, covered in blood seem to go right through the man next to him without even leaving a smear of the blood that now soaked his hand.

Turning back to the woman in his arms, he watched as her body went lifeless while he screamed again for someone, for anyone to help him.

"Cal? Can you hear me? Come on, Cal, calm down. I'm here. Can you hear me?" a voice said.

Calvin struggled to focus on the voice calling out to him. Perhaps that was the help he needed, but the voice he thought he was hearing wouldn't be in Colombia, South America with him. He was on a mission and far away from the glitz and glamour life his brother Cade lived, but he was quite positive that the voice now calling out to him was his Hollywood, superstar brother, Cade Weston. What would Cade be doing in Colombia, he thought? He looked around and didn't see him. Where was he? He tried to speak, but something painful was preventing him from making a sound. His throat felt like it was on fire. It felt blocked with something that was keeping him from speaking.

"Hold on, Cal, the doctor is coming," he heard.

The voice that time was Cameron's, his baby brother who shouldn't be in South America, but in Florida finishing up his last year of his undergraduate program before he started graduate school to continue with his advanced degree in Journalism. What was going on? Why are his brothers in South America and why weren't they coming to help him with the dying woman in his arms? He struggled to move and to talk, but could do neither. He felt helpless and weightless as if he was fighting against forces that wanted him to remain still, unable to do anything on his own.

"Mister Lymon, can you hear me? This is doctor Bell. Give me a minute and we'll get the tube out, but I need you to stop struggling with me."

Calvin could feel hands holding him down keeping him from moving.

"Everything's alright, Cal. You're alright, bro."

Cade? That was Cade's voice again, this time a lot closer than before. He wasn't hearing things. How could this be? Cade was in California or Texas or Florida or someplace else with his wife, Callie, but he definitely was not in South America.

"Cal, it's Cam – can you hear me? I'm here, I'm right here. We're all here and you're going to be okay."

Again, he heard Cameron's voice and he knew he must be in the twilight zone. All of a sudden, he felt his body jerk as he struggled to move and breathe. He felt like he was about to regurgitate, but it wasn't quite happening. He couldn't breathe even though he tried with all of his might to do so. Like a man trying to get his last breath, he inhaled and coughed as hard as he could as his eyes suddenly opened. His eyes did a quick, frightening scan and didn't recognize where he was. What frightened him most was he no longer had the beautiful woman in his arms. Where did she go?

"Breathe easy, Cal. Just breathe easy, bro. That's it."

Being able to see clearly now, he looked around and saw both of his brothers, a guy in a white coat and several other women surrounding him. Where was he?

"Calvin, it's doctor Bell. We took out your breathing tube and it's going to be a few minutes before you'll be able to speak and even then, it will be a strain. Can you look my way? Can you hear me? Do you understand me?"

Calvin couldn't take his eyes from his big brother, Cade. Wherever he was, he felt calmer knowing Cade was there, but he still needed to know why?

"Cade, talk to him. He seems to only want to focus on you," Dr. Bell said.

Cade walked closer to him and Calvin's eyes widened sensing something wasn't quite right.

"Hey, bro. You're woke. I know it's hard to talk and I can see you struggling to do so. The doctor said it's going to be hard, so just nod if you can understand me. Nod, Cal," Cade said sternly.

Shifting his eyes to the left he saw that standing next to Cade was Cameron who was also encouraging him to remain calm. Something was wrong if both of his brothers were standing over him and a doctor was talking to him. Was he in a bed?

Doing what Cade asked, he nodded. He looked to Cameron who cheered with excitement, no longer with a worried facial expression.

Calvin couldn't get his thoughts to line up to explain what was going on. One moment he was back in the bar with Sofia and then all of a sudden, she began bleeding from wounds and he couldn't help her. Sofia? Where was she? He already knew her name? Why was she bleeding like that on the day that they'd met which had been over a year ago? Was that right? He was so confused.

As his thoughts began to clear and the voices around him began to converse with each other, he thought back to a moment ago when he'd held

Sofia's lifeless body in his arms. He couldn't make sense of the scene that had played out. Sofia hadn't died in his arms in the pub and not on the day that they'd met. Now that his memory was clearing up, he remembered that she may not have died in his arms in the pub, but she had died and remembered seeing her body and being overwhelmed with grief.

He now knew that for a year and a half, he and Sofia had been in love and then it all ended the day she died. She was gone and the thought startled him. Something else was wrong as a sudden pain pierced his heart. They have a son! He and Sofia have a son and his name is Camico. Where was Camico? Sofia was dead, but where was their son? He'd promised her he'd look after Camico, but, where was he? If he was in a hospital or some facility where his brothers were and doctors and nurses were tending to him, where was his son? A feeling of trepidation overtook him as he tried with all of his might to form the words. With everything in him, he screamed at the top of his lungs.

"Camico!"

Everyone in the room turned toward him. Before he could decipher what was happening, where he was and when, the room went completely dark. Calvin had passed out.

CHAPTER TWO

Calvin drifted in and out of consciousness, still not fully aware of what was going on. He knew he was in a hospital and that he was in a lot of pain. His mind raced with thoughts of the path his life had taken to get him to this moment, in the hospital with bullet wounds that could result in his death. Taking his mind from the pain, he thought about what had gone wrong and if his decisions had been the right ones.

With all of the training he'd received over the years as a navy SEAL, Calvin knew the moment he'd crossed the line with Sofia Ramirez, the only daughter of the murderous drug lord, Valencio Ramirez, would be one that would change his life. He knew he would never betray his country for anything and so his only option was to get the job done that was assigned to him and his team and figure out what to do about Sofia before it was too late. The day he'd met her, something inside of him put aside what he knew he should have done, which was walk away.

He'd met the beautiful Sofia Ramirez during one of the times he and his SEAL team were sent to Colombia, South America to get intelligence on Valencio who had been under the watchful eye of the United States government for crimes he'd committed not just in South America, but also in the States. The drugs, the United States didn't care much about, but Valencio had been responsible for the murder of thousands of people, including some American politicians. Valencio's business was now an American problem and Calvin and his team of Navy SEALs were sent in to deal with him once and for all. The goal was to bring Valencio back to the U.S., but if for any reason, things turned bad, they would also take him dead.

Valencio's recruitment of American's to help bring his murderous rage to the United States was something no one was willing to tolerate. The man had billions which bought him a lot of entry into places he wouldn't be able to venture into if he was just a regular citizen of Colombia. Valencio was more than that. His rage had reached a level that made him not only a danger to the United States, but other countries when he started running high-powered, military-grade weapons that no person should have in their arsenal.

Calvin was leading a team into Colombia to take Valencio down once and for all, but first they needed to gather as much information as they could and if possible, get in good with members of Valencio's team. Little did Calvin know that while he and his team were enjoying some down time while in civilian clothes and doing reconnaissance to see what they were up against, he would set eyes on the most beautiful woman he'd ever seen. He had never swayed from his duty before, but something about Sofia drew him in.

The first time he'd seen her, he had been sitting outside of a pub enjoying a few drinks with his best friend, Mason. They were scheduled to head back to the United States in a little over a week when another SEAL team would take their place for a while. He had already been in South America for three months and his team needed a break. They were close to getting what they needed to deal with Valencio, but a little more intel was needed.

While they waited for the extraction plan, they were given a few days to relax and if any intel could be gathered, they were instructed to do it, but maintain a lowkey presence. Calvin knew his mistake was approaching Sofia, first because he couldn't take his eyes off of her and second to see if there was any information he could get from her, he had to get closer and not just in proximity. He had come across beautiful women before, but Sofia had something special and before he knew it, he was drawn in, putting both of their lives in danger. The plan was tight and secure, but they needed to verify and check out what they thought they knew. Sofia had been a mystery to him and the moment he knew exactly who she was from the history they were able to get on Valencio and the moment he saw her, he knew he was in trouble. She was even more beautiful than he expected. Now, seeing her in person, he was also intrigued on a personal level, something he would tell no one, not even Mason in the beginning.

According to sources, as a young girl, Sofia Ramirez had been sent away from Colombia after her mother was killed and her father wanted to keep her safe. It had been a coincidence that he'd met her that one day while having drinks at a pub. She had been back in Colombia for about a year, returning after years of being away and missing her father and older brother, Valentino.

As a young woman now, her father wanted her close to him and the only way to do that was to bring her back home. Valencio lived a dangerous life and along with his son, his second in command, he'd wreaked havoc across the world and something had to be done. What Calvin hadn't expected was how fast he would fall in love – a love that would change his life forever.

Sofia had been at the pub with friends that day, dancing and drinking and the moment his eyes connected with hers, he wanted her. He still remembered their first encounter.

"Hello."

Calvin looked up as the woman he'd been eyeing

all afternoon walked up to him. He'd first spotted her as he and Mason sat outside of the pub talking to a few of the locals when she walked by and entered the pub in a sexy white dress that hugged every one of her delicious curves. In an instant, she looked his way and their eyes locked. For a flash that lasted a second, she smiled at him and then turned back to her friends before they went inside before he could make his mouth form a hello in response. Against his better notion and against Mason's urging for them to not get too close, Calvin couldn't resist his next move which was to follow her inside of the dusty pub. He knew he was on his own time and a little fun was in store for his last seven days before returning to the states. He and his team wouldn't be called back in until there was enough information that would allow them to finally move in.

Getting up and walking into the pub, Calvin spotted the beauty and as she danced and twirled around, his eyes followed her every move. Surprising him, he watched her walk toward him and wasn't sure if she coming up to him or someone else. His heart practically stopped when she came to stop in front of him and said hello, again. This time he wouldn't falter when it came to answering. He smiled as looks of jealousy from every man in the pub who had been looking at her hoping to get the chance to meet her, seared through him. He like everyone else was mesmerized by the beauty in white, but it appeared, as with him, she had eyes for him as he had for her.

"Hello to you," he said in response to the hello she'd said to him before they entered the pub.

"I'm Sofia and you've been watching me," she said in a sweet, sexy, soft tone.

Calvin leaned back in his chair, crossing one leg over his knee. Before answering, he took a perusal of her body from the bottom up and when his eyes landed on her dark, sinful glaring eyes, he already knew he was done for.

"I was watching you and you said hello to me. I hope I didn't make you uncomfortable by staring at you. You're very beautiful and trust me, I'm not the only person watching you. I'm sure you get that kind of attention everywhere you go," he said.

She smiled and his heart skipped a beat.

"I do and I usually ignore it or they end up ignoring me when they find out who my father is," she said.

"Is your father that scary?" Calvin asked, going along as if he didn't know who her father was.

When she looked at him sideways, he knew that she was trying to figure him out because everyone in Colombia knew her father and in fact, everyone in South America knew her father.

Eying her, he'd studied enough about her and had seen photos of her as part of the research into who Valencio was, but the photos had been from a *few years back when she was a young girl. Now, a full-fledged woman, she was incredibly beautiful. Seeing the photos of her was nothing compared to encountering her in person now as a woman.*

"Let's just say, he pulls a lot of weight and a few times when word got back to him that some guy pushed up on me, it didn't go so well for him. In fact, I'm not sure I ever saw him again. I wouldn't want that to happen to you," she said sheepishly.

"Well, fathers don't scare me and I'm assuming you're a grown woman and not just a girl who looks like a grown woman," he said, doing everything he could to not let on that he knew all about her. "You are positively beautiful," he added.

Sofia swung her long black hair from around one shoulder to the other and looked him straight in the eyes.

"I'm all grown, inside and out and at twenty-three, soon to be twenty-four, I like to decide who I find interesting enough to say hello to. I waited for you to make a move, but you didn't which is why I'm now standing in front of you. Thank you for saying I'm beautiful. I came over to tell you that I find you handsome and wondered if you were ever going to say anything to me considering you said nothing outside when I said hello," Sofia said, unashamed of her boldness.

"Well, I'm only here for a few more days and I wouldn't want to approach someone as beautiful as you if I wasn't going to be around long enough

to get to know them," he said.

Sofia leaned down close to his ear.

"A lot can happen in a few days. Sometimes a few days is better than no days at all," she said standing back up to her full height. "An entire lifetime can be lived in just a few days," she added and smiled.

"Whew, I think I'm already in love. I love bold woman who speak their mind," he said.

"In that case, why don't you tell me your name so that you don't continue to be nameless around me and then perhaps the man who doesn't have a name yet will ask me to dance," she said.

"My name is Leo," Calvin lied. He knew to think quick when it came to sharing any personal information. At all times, he was a United States Navy SEAL on a mission and he couldn't allow himself to be compromised for a pretty face.

"Leo. I like that and it fits you. Leo's remind me of lions, big, strong and powerful. Is that you, Leo?" she asked.

Calvin stood from the table. "I like to think so."

When Mason cleared his throat, Calvin turned, remembering he was sitting there. Once Sofia walked up to him, he couldn't remember anything. She was already having an effect on him that made him forget about his best friend.

"Hello," Sofia said to Mason.

"This is Carl," Calvin said. "He and I are visiting and decided to enjoy the atmosphere here at the pub."

"Well, it's nice to meet you, Carl. My friend Antonia over there in the denim jean shorts likes you. She's shy and was scared to come over with me," Sofia said.

Mason looked from Sofia to Calvin and tried to warn Calvin with his eyes to not forget why there were in South America.

"I'm sure Carl wouldn't mind going over to say hello to your friend while you and I dance," Calvin said, directing his comment directly at Mason.

Mason stood and shook Sofia's hand to shake it.

"It's nice to meet you, Sofia and I think I will go over and say hello to Antonia."

Mason let his eyes linger on Calvin a few extra minutes letting him know he wasn't feeling the direction their day was going in. He knew Calvin was treading on dangerous ground and had a feeling even one dance would be a mistake. They not only worked together but were best friends and if he trusted anyone and anything, it was Calvin and his judgement, so he let her reservations go for the moment.

After Mason walked away, Calvin turned back to Sofia.

"Now, would you like to dance?" he asked.

Sofia smiled. "I thought you'd never ask."

Calvin remembered that they danced until the pub closed and the owner threw them out. Instead of going back to join the rest of his team, he stood outside and talked to Sofia until she finally had to get back home before her father or brother came looking for her. A smarter man would have let her walk away and let their one night of dancing be enough, but he couldn't. Sofia was too hard to resist. He whispered to her that he wanted to see her again and they agreed to meet the next day for lunch. That lunch date turned into a dinner date later that evening and three days later, she was like a drug he couldn't resist.

What he didn't know was that Sofia had been sneaking away to see him. During their last two days together, she revealed that her father had been questioning where she was going for those few days without having any security around her. She has raised her father's suspicious eye.

During one of their times together, she revealed to him how dangerous her father actually was. Calvin didn't care because in a few short days, he'd fallen hard for her and he didn't care that her father was a dangerous man and no one knew that better than him. The assignment he was on had information on him regarding the number of dead bodies tied to him, some he'd taken out directly himself. Valencio Ramirez was a heinous creature, no longer someone he would consider a man. This was someone who'd had his own wife, Valentina, Sofia's mother, killed back when Sofia was a little girl because she'd turned against him, something he discovered Sofia had no clue about.

He and Sofia fell in love quick and by his last two days before leaving, they hated being apart from each other. Outside of a little touching and feeling and a whole lot of kissing, they hadn't gone any further. Calvin felt bad that he wasn't able to tell her his real name and come clean about who he was, which is why he kept things between them from getting intimate though they both wanted to. He knew he was leaving soon and didn't know if he'd ever see her again. With everything in him, he wanted to. He couldn't imagine not being around her again. They wanted to be closer and though he wanted to take the lead on that, he was surprised when Sofia planned a quiet, romantic night for them at Antonia's apartment. She and Mason didn't hit it off, but Antonia was key in helping with his time with Sofia and for that, Calvin was grateful.

Valencio knew that Sofia and Antonia had been friends ever since she returned to Colombia and it wasn't odd for her to spend the night or sometimes an entire weekend with Antonia. Valencio made sure to have security around her when he was away on what he called business, but he let up when she hung with friends, hoping she would blend in and not stand out too much as the daughter of Valencio Ramirez.

While Valencio and his son had taken a flight out of the country, he was glad that she would be spending the weekend with Antonia and had no idea the weekend would actually be spent with him.

She'd set everything up from a candlelit dinner to sexy dancing. The dancing led them to the bedroom where he made love to her through the rest of the night and discovered that he had been her first lover.

Thinking Antonia was coming back once daylight came, Calvin thought their time together was over. He was delighted to hear that they would have the whole day and night to themselves, again. Antonia was spending time with a man she liked, giving them her apartment the whole time. They spent that day indoors talking, cooking and making love.

Calvin knew he only had a few hours left and didn't like leaving her and promised he would return when he could. Sofia wanted to stay in touch, but Calvin talked her out of it in case her father caught on. He didn't want to leave her to deal with his wrath. He wasn't sure when he'd be able to get back to see her knowing that he had a job to do. He needed to see if he had any leave coming up and instead of visiting with his brothers, Cade and Cameron, something he tried to do whenever he had time away from being a SEAL, he wanted to take that time to see Sofia if he could. His brothers would understand and lived busy lives themselves. Only Mason knew about him and Sofia and as far as he was concerned, she was worth the risk of returning to South America for pleasure and not business.

His brother Cade Weston, a Hollywood actor and businessman was living the life at the top of the movie box office, he was producing several television shows, all airing on Wednesday nights, making it the hottest night of watching television while also securing his spot at the top of the clothing industry with his hot line of men's apparel, especially hats. He'd won one award after the other and was already working on the next big movie where he was able to co-produce with Will Smith where the expectation was that it would be one of the highest grossing movies of the year. He'd recently fallen in love with a beautiful woman, Callie and to say she was perfect for him would be an understatement. Cade Weston was not only his brother, but also his hero.

Cade had changed his last name from Lymon to Weston years ago in order to transition into the entertainment industry and he prepared for making it big by keeping the spotlight off of his family as much as possible. He was the one who wanted to be a star and didn't want his family on any paparazzi radars.

After his career as an actor took off, he was given the nickname "Heartthrob" because of the impact he had on women. After years of playing the field, he was surprised that Cade had actually found a woman he was willing to give up his playboy ways for. Now that he himself had met Sofia, he knew what that kind of love was like. After only a few days, he would give anything to always have the love he was sharing with Sofia.

Cameron, the youngest of the three of them was a college student studying sports management and communications, but Calvin had a feeling he wasn't going to stick to sports management too much longer. Like Cade, Cameron liked attention and the last time they spoke, he talked about a career in television himself.

Like Cade, he told Cameron, he didn't care what career he chose as long as he stayed in college and graduated. Cade had gone into this career after high school and he'd gone into the military. Cameron would be the first to get a college degree and as his brothers, they made sure he stayed on task.

The three of them had grown up close after having a mom and dad that weren't good parents. When they could no longer care for three boys, they were sent to live with their grandparents who loved and spoiled them.

Growing up in Compton with two drug addicted parents was a far cry from the loving and encouraging life they lived with their grandparents. They nurtured them to live productive lives and if it had not been for them, there was no telling what would become of the three Lymon brothers.

Being the big brother, Cade had always looked out for them and they checked in with each other often.

With his career as a navy SEAL, Calvin found

himself all over the world and Cade was adamant that they be able to reach each other at any time. Being a SEAL and knowing how effective satellite phones are and how far the range would be, Cade secured three phones for them and they had an emergency code. It was there ray of dropping everything and coming together if they needed to. So far, none of them had to use the code, though he did use his satellite phone when he was in an area that did not get regular cellular phone service.

One directive from Cade is that they were never to be without their phones. If he had leave coming up, he needed to call Cade to let him know that he was doing good, but that he wouldn't be coming to visit. His plan was to find a way to get back to Sofia, even if for a few days. After all, it was her who said a lot could be done with just a few days. The fact that they were as close as they were after a few days proved how true that statement was. He left her that last day sad and unsure of the next time he'd see her but promised her he would try to get back to her soon.

Sofia had cried when he left and he was glad that Antonia had returned to be that friend when he had to leave her alone. When he left South America, he also left his heart there. He also knew nothing would keep him from getting back to her as soon as he could. He had already risked so much getting involved with her, so in his opinion, he didn't have much else to lose. He was wrong.

As he lay awake in his hospital bed, listening to the beeps of all of the equipment he was hooked up to, Calvin tried to recall all that he knew had happened eighteen months ago from Sofia's perspective. His mind raced with the chilling details she'd shared with him about her life while he was away from her until the day when his life changed forever.

CHAPTER THREE
18 months ago

Sofia was nervous. Her world was about to be turned upside down as soon as her father discovered her secret, a secret she wouldn't be able to keep from him much longer.

Her father liked total control of everything and everyone in his space and that included his two children. She and older brother, Valentino, who had been named after their father and their mother, Valentina, were the only family that mattered to her father. He didn't trust his own family and her mother's family didn't like or trust him.

She missed her mother. Valentina died when Sofia was six years old and the only explanation she'd been given is that her mother had taken ill while on a trip and she never recovered. As she grew older, she questioned that story when she really began missing her. It was through her mother's family that she learned the story she'd been told may not be the correct one. It was the story her father told her and Valentino and though she had a hard time dealing with it, her brother was hard-nosed like their father. He never showed much emotion even at the age of thirteen, learning of their mother's death. He was already becoming a mini version of their hardcore father.

Not knowing what her father actually did to take care of their family, she was kept far away from a lot of secret meetings he often had at their house, which was more like a compound. It was a large, complex house with sixteen bedrooms, twenty bathrooms, three kitchens, two swimming pools, one indoors and one outdoors, a tennis court, basketball court, bowling alley and a large gym, where she loved spending her time practicing gymnastics and dancing. It had been her dream to be a professional gymnast, but that never happened though she still enjoyed the workout.

As a young girl, one day while she was working on the uneven bars, there was a commotion at the house and one of the men who guarded them day and night came in and told her to stay in the room. When she heard the lock click after he left, she knew it had to be serious. She could hear men running around screaming and she thought she'd heard gunfire. Afraid, she grabbed a lot of the mats that were on the gym floor together and made a fort for herself where she hid until her father came looking for her. That was the same day he had sent her to live far away from him and her brother. He had cousins who lived in Mexico and she'd lived with them until after her twenty-second birthday when she moved back to Colombia to be closer to her father and brother.

Both of them had changed over the years and when she returned, she thought they would be a typical family, but that wasn't the case.

She read a lot about her father in the newspaper articles and on the internet after hearing whispers about his dealings from family. Valencio Ramirez was a dangerous man, accused of dealing large quantities of drugs and taking the life of anyone who crossed him. There had been talk that her mother's death wasn't from any illness, but was at the hands of her own father, something she refused to believe. He wouldn't do that. She loved her mother and from what she remembered, they loved each other. They fought like a lot of people did, but for him to take her life, she couldn't grasp that and hadn't thought about it again after she begged him to allow her to come home. Wanting her closer, he agreed.

There was one occasion where she witnessed her father's rage. At sixteen, she was in school in Mexico when the brother of one of her friends, who was twenty-five, took a liking to her. She hadn't encouraged it and didn't like the attention and ended up telling her family about it. A few days later, he father showed up in Mexico and asked her about this guy he'd heard about who made her feel uncomfortable. She didn't think much of it and gave him the information he asked for. A few days later while in class, her friend stopped coming to school. She decided to stop at the friend's house one day after school and found the entire family had moved. When she asked a neighbor, she was told that the son, the one that had his eye on her, had turned up dead with his inner organs cut out and laying on the ground beside him. The story was that some men came and took him away over some girl he'd been harassing. The next they heard the family was given a day to move away and never speak of it.

The more she tried to find out, the more people kept information from her. It wasn't until she was about to move back to Colombia years later that one of her cousins told her to reconsider going. He warned her that she had no idea the kind of life her father lived back in Colombia and that she didn't want to be anywhere near it.

He proceeded to tell her to remember what happened to that boy she told everyone was creeping her out and how within a few days of her father arriving, that boy was found murdered. His tongue had been sent back to his family with a note that said he should have watched who he messed with and talked to and that he would never be talking again. It wasn't until his sister, her friend, told the family about his pursuit of Sofia that everyone put two and two together and came up with this boy had been on the other end of Valencio Ramirez's wrath. Her cousin told her that her father was a dangerous man and the stories that she'd read were all true. She was anxious to get back to her home in Colombia and ignored the warning.

After returning, there were many secret meetings that didn't include her. Her brother was as cold and hard as their father and whenever she was around him, she didn't like the vibe. She was told she could never go anywhere without someone from their security detail with her. Thankfully, she was able to convince her father that she would be fine when she was with her friends. She asked if the detail could be around, but unseen and her father agreed to that. He wanted her to have fun and seemed happy that she didn't want to stay in the house all the time. It was where he conducted a lot of his business.

She'd been home for less than a year and in that time, had seen first-hand who her father really was. She would eavesdrop on his meetings when she could, knowing that she could hear a lot through the vent in the room below her father's office. She heard details about his drug dealings, murder for hire and other odious crimes he committed. There were guns and security men with guns in their house around the clock. Staff were sworn to secrecy and often paid huge sums of money for their silence.

Money was never a problem in their house. There were rooms full of money, safes full of money and weapons and in a hidden panel in the closet of her bedroom, there were two large foot lockers full of large bills. Her father once told her that money was hers, but she needed to access and spend it wisely and not get on anyone's radar with her spending. She had cars at her disposal after one of the security guards taught her how to drive. She'd asked her father, but he was too busy. He and her brother spent a lot of time away from the house at another of Valencio's compounds in Colombia. He wanted to keep attention away from the house now that she was in it.

Life changed for her when she moved back to Colombia. She found new friends and spent a lot of her time with her newfound friends, partying, shopping and having fun. Though her father never allowed any of her friends to spend the night in their house, he was lenient and allowed her to spend nights away from home as long as he knew he could keep her safe. He told her that there were bad men who would love to use her as a pawn in a game to get back at him, so she needed to be careful. He taught her how to use a gun and she knew where they were located throughout the house, in every room in case it was needed.

Life was more like a prison than not until the day she met Leo at the pub. The moment she saw him sitting at a table outside of the pub she and Antonia loved going to, she couldn't keep her eyes off of him. She'd seen him from a distance a time or two before, but this time, he was able to see her.

That day, he was dressed in blue denim jeans and a blue denim t-shirt under a white linen collared leisure shirt. She thought she could see a necklace of some type under his shirt, but he kept it hidden. When they were together, he never wore it.

That day at the pub, she'd fallen in love instantly. She watched him watch her from across the room and waited for him to approach her, something he didn't do. If she was going to meet him, she had to make her own move. Walking over to him, she kept her eyes on his handsome face. There were a lot of men who approached her often, but she never had a mutual interest until Leo walked into her life.

After that first day, she asked Antonia to help her spend more time with him. Using her as an excuse was the only way she would be able to get away from the house as often as she needed to. Luckily, her father and brother had to leave on a last-minute trip and she and Leo were able to spend two glorious days in each other's arms. With him, she experienced her first time making love and it was magical.

Leo was gentle and made her body burn for his touch time after time. Once she told him that she was a virgin, he took his time and showed her how a woman should be loved. He kissed her like she was a precious jewel. He touched her like he would never get enough of her feel. He loved her as if it was the last time they would be together. He gave her all of him and in turn, she gave him all of her. There love was a whirlwind and the two days ended much too early.

Now, it had been two months since she'd last seen Leo and he'd sent word to her that he was returning in a few days to see her. She was more than ready to see him and to share something with him she hoped he wouldn't be upset with her about as she knew her father was going to be. In seven months, she and Leo were going to have a baby. She was pregnant and happy about it. Her biggest dilemma is telling her father and hoping he didn't take any type of brutal action against Leo for getting his only daughter pregnant.

From the minute she found out, she'd been on a high and anxiously awaiting her baby's birth. First, she needed to prepare for Leo's return by contacting Antonia to get help with her plan to secretly meet with him. For the first time in her life, she was ready to put her life in South America behind and hopefully spend the rest of her life with Leo. The few times he was able to get letters to her, he expressed how much he loved her and wanted them to have a life together. She wanted that, too even if it meant leaving her brother and father behind.

CHAPTER FOUR

"Hey, Cal. How many days are you off, dude?" Mason asked.

"Seven and I intend to make the most out of every day," Calvin said as he changed clothes after working out in the gym. He and Mason had been at the gym all day, something they did every week as time permitted. As a SEAL, one of the most important aspects of what they did required them to stay in the best shape possible which means lots of hours in the gym.

"Is what I hear in your voice a plan to visit Cade or Cameron or a special beauty in South America? I'm hoping it's not the latter. Dangerous grounds you're treading on," Mason said.

Calvin turned around and faced him square on.

"I hear you, but I'm telling you, those few days with her were some of the best in my life. I've never met anyone like her, even with the five-year age difference. It's a shame she has a father who happens to be one of the most notorious people to ever walk the face of this earth. What he couldn't do was forget about Sofia.

"Does she know who you really are? Does she know why you were in South America and that you knew who she was before she even walked over to you? I understand that you're in love with her. I could see it the moment you laid eyes on her and I couldn't be happier for you. I know you've had your struggles over having some kind of personal life. It's hard to do because we're gone so often, but this girl is the one you fall in love with? The one whose father is our target? What's going to happen when she finds out who you are after her father is captured or killed? Perhaps you never plan on telling her that. What do you plan to do? Bring her back to the States for a life with you? What are you planning, another rendezvous with her in a country you shouldn't be in without the proper protection? I'm concerned for your safety. I thought maybe you'd have some fun and move on beyond it, but that didn't happen. I should have known since I've seen what your interest in women looks like and from the start, I knew this was different."

Calvin exhaled and knew what Mason was saying, but he was leading with his heart. Sofia was already a major part of his life.

"It is different. You know how I've been with women, keeping things casual and if I see them, then I see them and if I don't, there's no harm done. Sofia is different and after that one week of getting to know her, I am in love with her. I've been thinking about this and the impact on what my job is and I don't see a big issue."

"Dude, if what you're planning is some kind of happily ever after with her, what's going to happen when she finds out your name isn't Leo and that you work for the United States military, in that country to either secure or take out her father? There are so many ways this could go wrong and I'm concerned. As your team mate and the one person who is as close to you as one of your brothers, I'm telling you to walk away from this. Have your fun, but walk away and forget about her."

Calvin looked over at Mason who grabbed what he needed from his own locker and prepared to head home.

"You have the love of your life to go home to when we have down time. I know how you feel about Stacy and I'm glad you're happy. I never thought I'd find a woman who made me think about forever, but Sofia does. I haven't thought beyond my feelings for her and I'm clear on the mission for when we'll need to return and take down Valencio. By then, I hope to have a plan in place for dealing with Sofia, but right now, I need to see her and since it's my off-time, I'm not thinking about it in terms of work. You know me, so you know if I'm willing to risk everything, Sofia means everything to me. I know I need to come clean with her, but for now, I just need to see her again. I'm sure there will be repercussions for me with the powers that be, but I am focused and I know I have a job to do. When the time comes, I will still do that. During my time away from here and with her, I will still have clarity of my loyalties and they are and always will be with my country. Valencio Ramirez is a horrible person, but I'm already in love with his daughter and there's nothing I can do about that," Calvin confessed.

"I hear you, bro. I can see your love for her every time you speak her name. All I want is for you to be careful. One word from anyone there to Valencio about you and your life is at risk and possibly the lives of those close to you," Mason warned.

He looked around to be sure no one else was around to hear what he was about to say. He walked over closer to Calvin to speak quieter. Calvin looked around like Mason was doing, wondering what he was checking for.

"You checking for someone?" Calvin asked.

"Yeah, for any other ears in here. Listen, you and I have talked about this for a while, but keep in mind, someone on our side is aiding Valencio. The things he's allowed to do and how he can easily get in and out of the United States is because he's got men on this side. When you and I tossed ideas back and forth, what did we come up with?" Mason asked, hoping to jog Calvin's memory on how serious the situation was.

"That a higher authority in the military or in the

U.S. government is on Valencio's payroll."

"Right. Remember that as you're traipsing around that country with his daughter thinking you're enjoying downtime. There is no such thing for an American soldier in a foreign land, especially one where Valencio lives. Remember that. Send me word that you're okay on a daily basis or I'll be on the first flight to South America to look for you. Watch your back. Valencio is smart and if his daughter feels anything for you like you feel for her, she won't be able to hide it. You know how he is with any guy checking for his beautiful daughter. You won't be an exception to his wrath."

Calvin nodded his head in agreement. He had to remember to not only lead by his heart if he were going to stay off of Valencio's radar. He was not only risking his life, but also the mission.

"I hear you and it's all noted. I'll only be there a few days and then it's back here to join the team. I'll keep an eye on my back and I'll be in touch. Now, I need to all Cade to let him know I'm not joining him for my time off," Calvin said reaching for his phone.

Mason grabbed his things and walked out of the gym leaving Calvin alone with his thoughts.

Calvin knew it was wrong to get involved with Sofia. He had a plan to connect with Sofia and South America was large. If things worked out well, he would get in, spend some time with her and then get back home. He wanted her to know that he wanted her out of South America and away from Valencio. Living the life he laid out for her was not one that would keep her alive, he feared. He reached for his phone to call Cade. He needed to handle that first.

"Hey, bro!" Calvin exclaimed the minute Cade answered.

"Cal! What's happening. I'm surprised to hear from you. How are things going? Any secret missions you still can't share with me?" Cade quipped.

"Right! You got jokes. I can never share a mission, but nothing major is happening at the moment. In fact, I have a week off for some down time," he said.

"Does that mean you're coming to California for a visit? I'd love to see my brother who has been missing in action for almost a year now," Cade said.

"I told you I was going on an assignment and I'd be gone for a while. I'll be going back in a few months to wrap this last assignment up. Sorry, I won't be visiting you this time."

"Are you visiting Cameron or going home to see the grandparents?" he asked.

Calvin knew he was going to be hit with a barrage of questions the minute he said he wasn't visiting him in California. He tried to get time in with family as often as he could, but this time, he had other plans.

"Not this time. I'm going out of the country for a

few days to visit a friend," Calvin said and then waited for more questions. He didn't have to wait long.

"Friend? In another country? Is this friend of the female persuasion? How serious is this if you're taking time you would normally spend with us to go out of the country?" Cade asked.

"Yes, it's a female and it actually is pretty serious and believe me, I'm surprising myself. I met her and fell in love instantly."

"I can relate to that," Cade said.

"I know you can. How's Callie?" Calvin asked.

"She's great and I'm looking forward to making her my wife soon. I hope you'll be coming home for the wedding."

"Now Cade, you know I would never miss that as long as I'm not on an assignment. Let me know the when and where and I'll put the time in."

"Sounds like a plan. Now, tell me if I'll be able to meet this woman soon. I can feel the love in your words," Cade asked.

"Calvin! You're being summoned. Sarge is looking for you and he doesn't seem happy," a voice behind him called out.

"Definitely, but right now, I have to get going. I'm being called by my sergeant and when they call, they expect us to run which is what I need to do. I'll give you a call when I get back. We'll talk more then. I wanted you to know that I'd be on leave in case you need me. I'll have my satellite with me.

Where I'm going may be remote and I may not be able to get a regular cell signal."

"Alright, be safe and I'll let Cameron know you called."

"I appreciate that and congrats on the wedding and finding that perfect woman. Cameron told me what happened when he came to visit you and what a mix-up that caused when you almost lost Callie for good. He said you put your knee pads on and tracked her down to beg her to forgive you. I had to have him tell me the story twice before I was convinced my playboy brother was hooked on one woman. I bet the women in Hollywood are disappointed you're off the market!" Calvin supposed.

"Well, Callie isn't any other woman and when I found her, I knew she was the one, just like you and your new lady."

"Calvin, now!" he heard his sergeant call.

"I better go this time. That was actually my sergeant calling for me. Love you, bro."

"Love you, too, Calvin and remember to be careful. Watch your back."

"I will."

Calvin hung up and went in the direction of the howling voice of his commanding officer. He hoped it wasn't something that would delay his trip to South America to see Sofia. He didn't want anything to keep him from her any longer. Two months was long enough without much contact other than a few short phone calls and a few emails. He didn't want to risk reaching out to her knowing Valencio was her father. All the sneaking around they had done the last time he was there was risky enough, but he didn't want any trace of him on Valencio's radar. He was already risking enough for love and all he wanted was to hold Sofia in his arms again.

CHAPTER FIVE
Eighteen Months Later

Valencio Ramirez paced in his office as he waited for the men he sent out on a mission to finish gathering in his office, hopefully with good news. He was tired of waiting. How hard could it be to find someone.

"What's the word on the streets?" Valencio asked.

"No word at all. I haven't been able to get anything on any guy named Leo. Whoever he is, he's not in this country anymore. Are you sure Sofia isn't lying about who Camico's father is? I mean, I can't find anyone who knows who this Leo character is."

Valencio fumed when he didn't get the information he was expecting to get. He wanted to know who got his daughter pregnant and then left her to take care of the baby alone.

For over a year since the moment Sofia divulged that she was pregnant, he'd been unable to get her to give him any information about this man. His daughter was closed lip about who Leo was and even after questioning everyone she knew, no one else knew either. He thought he would be able to convince Antonia to tell him the truth, but according to her, whoever Sofia had been seeing, she'd kept it to herself. He had no option, but to trust that. Sofia, on the other hand, had more explaining to do. He was infuriated that his daughter could keep something like this from him for so long.

"Keep checking. This mystery person had to exist at one time. My daughter didn't get pregnant through immaculate conception. She's protecting this guy, probably afraid of what I'd do to him and she's right to do so. As soon as I find this guy, he'll wish he'd never been born. The only good thing out of all of this is my grandson, Camico. That nine-month-old bundle of happiness is everything to me. Throw more money at people and see what you can find," Valencio said, sending his contacts away.

The minute his office door opened, he expected to hear it close, but instead he heard the whimpers of his grandson.

"There's Poppy," Sofia said as she walked into his office with Camico in her arms.

Valencio lit up, forgetting about the fact that his daughter, who he thought told him everything, kept a secret as big as who Camico's father was from him.

"There's my big boy," Valencio said walking over to her and taking Camico from her arms.

"I'm about to put him down for a nap and thought I'd stop in here first," she explained.

"I'm glad you did. I missed him this week while I was away. He looks bigger," Valencio acknowledged.

"He's getting bigger every day," Sofia said. She smiled though inside she was worried. She knew who the men were who had left her father's office as she arrived. She had been hearing from friends that her father was still trying to get a lead on Leo. The only thing she was willing to share was a first name and nothing else, knowing that even that name wouldn't lead him to anyone. She couldn't believe that after all this time, he was still looking. She was more thankful for Antonia than ever. She was the only person who knew about Leo and what his true identity was.

"Are you ever going to tell me the truth about his father?" Valencio asked, while playing with the baby. He never looked at her when he asked her about Camico's father knowing anything coming out of her mouth wouldn't be the truth.

His daughter isn't who he thought or hoped she'd be. Something changed in her halfway through her pregnancy. She used to have a gleam in her eyes when she saw him, especially when he and his son were away on business and returned. She was no longer his little girl and lately, she'd been more distant than ever. She was becoming more like her mother than he liked.

Valentina had been his world and he thought he was her world. He was heartbroken to find that she had been working with law enforcement to bring down his empire. She was feeding them information about his inner workings and as much as it killed him inside, he had to deal with her the same way he would deal with any other traitor. Every time he looked at Sofia, he saw her mother. Sofia was now the age that her mother was when he'd first met her.

"Poppy, I don't know what you mean. I told you his name was Leo Carter, an American. I never told him I was pregnant. I fell for him fast and we were careless that one time we had sex. I'm not a child and I wasn't when I met him. Camico is nine months old and you and I have been having this conversation since I first told you I was pregnant. At this point, I don't think it matters. We love Camico and he is a happy, healthy little wonder. I can't imagine my life without him and the fact that his father knows nothing about him is fine with me. You need to let it go," she said.

"Let what go?" Valentino said entering the office.

Sofia turned at the sound of her brother's voice and knew the conversation she had hoped was over was about to get deeper. Her father found an ally in Valentino when it came to questioning her about Camico's father.

"Your sister still won't give me more information about this guy who knocked her up and then disappeared," Valencio said.

"What's the big secret, sis?" Valentino asked. "Hey, Camico," he said taking him from his father's arms.

"It's not a secret. I have told you both a million times that he was someone who had been visiting and everything happened quickly. He's from the United States and was here on some kind of vacation or something and we hooked up."

"Sofia, Ramirez women do not hook up!" Valencio screamed. He could feel himself age every time she said the words. He wanted more for his only daughter than to be a hookup for some American guy. The more he thought about it, the more he wanted to kill him.

"Oh, Poppy. Calm down before you pop a blood vessel. I am my own woman and clearly your assessment isn't true because that's exactly what I did." She turned to Valentino. "Now, hand me my son because he's overdue for his afternoon nap."

She used Camico's little hand to wave to her father.

"You know we'll find him," Valentino said.

Sofia ignored him.

"Tell Poppy bye, bye, Mico," she said before turning to leave the room, closing the door behind her.

"You know she's lying right, Poppy?" Valentino said.

Valencio sat down behind his desk.

"I know she is and there's something about this whole thing I still don't like. Who was this American she laid down with and then let him walk away like she meant nothing to him? That's unacceptable. My American contacts can't find anything either," he said.

"Sofia is strong-minded and stubborn," Valentino said.

"She's too much like your mother was and I don't like it."

"You know, Basser said he caught her snooping around in here while we were away."

Valencio was shocked when he returned from a trip abroad to hear that his daughter had been seen in his office going through his cabinets and looking at files. Basser, one of the security guys thought he saw her taking pictures of something with her cell phone. Not surprisingly when he asked her about her cell phone, she told him she'd lost it when she went into Panama to visit Antonia and didn't know where it was. By the time he returned, she'd already picked up a new one. He tried to have a trace put on the phone to track where it was, but he got nothing. His daughter was acting suspicious.

"I know and I haven't gotten a straight answer on that. She told me she wasn't snooping. She was in here looking for something that belonged to Camico that she thought was in here. I don't know what that could have been."

"What do you think is going on with her?"

Valentino asked.

"I don't know, but we'll keep a closer eye on her. Now, let's talk business. How are we coming along with the gun shipment? Is everything all set?"

"We are, though we have a small problem. Somehow, the authorities found out about the first shipment and took possession before they got to our hands. Luckily, the second and third weren't on anyone's radar."

"We have a leak somewhere and our sources are backing off because word is out that officials are closing in on us. I don't know how so much information about our dealings is getting out into the public and I don't like it. We need to seal that leak up and do it immediately. I don't like anything affecting my money. We've made some big deals predicated on our ability to get those shipments out of here and into the United States. Let's talk about what's next. Gather the team together for a meeting in an hour here in my office. I want to grill all of them to be sure no one of them are snitches. If we find a leak, I want him dealt with immediately. Is that clear?" Valencio said.

"Crystal clear, Pop. I'll have everyone here. Are we going to the other house? I know you try not to conduct too much business here, especially now with Camico in the house," Valentino asked.

"Let's plan on doing that tomorrow. Tonight, I want to sit down and talk to Sofia to find out what's going on with her. Her behavior has been off-kilter and I want to get a handle on it. Make sure there's a detail with her at all times when she leaves here."

"I'm on it, Pop."

Valentino left the office and turned toward his sister's wing of the house. Maybe he could get more information from her than his father has been able to get.

CHAPTER SIX

Sofia finally laid Camico down in his crib. He'd been fussy for over an hour and she knew it was because he hadn't had his usual afternoon nap. Her plan was to leave the house to go into town to connect with Calvin so that he could spend some time with Camico. They hadn't been able to communicate much and never when her father and brother were at the house. The last thing she wanted to do was risk Calvin's safety. She loved him too much to have anything happen to him.

Again, thankful to Antonia and a few of her other close friends, she was able to sneak quiet time with her, Calvin and Camico together as a family, though those times weren't long visits because she knew her father had men watching her. Calvin had been back several times throughout her pregnancy and now that he was back to wrap up his work, they were making plans to get her and Camico out of South America. She wanted her life to be with Calvin in the United States and far away from her father.

She couldn't believe the changes in her life since she'd met him Calvin. After their love affair that one week, he returned to see her two months later and before he could get out a single word when they met up at Antonia's apartment, she blurted out to him that she was pregnant. She had paused, waiting for his reaction and hoped it would be a happy one. It turned out that Calvin was happier than she was. Later that night as they laid in bed together and he laid his head on her chest and rubbed her flat stomach, her love for him blossomed even more if that were possible. They had only communicated a few times after he left for the states. He was able to get a message to her when he knew he would be returning and she'd been excited.

As they laid together after making love and enjoyed a quiet night by candlelight, the man she'd been calling Leo for months revealed a secret to her. He told her first, that he loved her and couldn't be happier about the baby. He also told her that though his love for her was real, his name was not. For the remainder of the night when they should have been sleeping, they stayed up talking and he told her who he was. She then understood his reason for being in South America. There was a lot about his mission that he couldn't reveal to her, but he did tell her that her father was the target and that he was a very bad man, something she had learned for herself.

Calvin felt bad that he couldn't share more with her, but his first priority was his allegiance to his country. His second was his love for her and their unborn baby. He didn't reveal his last name, just his first name and the fact that he was in the United States military. She didn't press for him to tell her more because all she needed to know was that he loved her and loved their child; that was enough for her. She meant it when she told him she would never do anything that could risk his life or his mission.

She also shared a few secrets of her own, starting with her father's unsavory business. She offered to help him in any way she could, but Calvin was unbending when he said that he did not want her involved in any kind of way. She tried to explain that she could find out information for him and help him in his efforts, but he again stressed the fact that she needed to remain safe and think about their child.

After that one week together, he had to return to the states and when she was seven months pregnant, he returned, this time on assignment. They weren't able to spend nights together, but when she could get away for a few hours, they met secretly in a lot of different places because by then, her father had people watching her closely. Thankfully, Calvin knew how to blend in and plan clandestine meetings that threw off the trail of any of her father's men who were following her.

Once she had Camico, she was able to get pictures of the baby to him and then they arranged to meet so that he could set eyes on his son.

So much had happened in the time that they'd known each other and even though he told her to stay away from her father's business, she told him a few things she'd learned by listening to some of his meetings through the vent in his office, something she discovered as a little girl exploring the house.

Below her father's office was a big storage area and in one corner, there was a vent and when her father held meetings, she could hear everything from that room. Now that she was older, she tried to get to that space more often, typically when Camico was asleep and his nanny would keep an eye on him.

A lot of her father's meetings were held at the other house he owned, a place she was barred from going to. The little information she was able to gather, she shared. Calvin thought she was taking too many risks and asked her to stop. His team would get what they needed and they would be able to live their lives together openly. His plan was to take her and the baby to the United States to live. He was already working on getting a passport for Camico with the information and papers she was able to get to him. Standing in their way was her father and brother and soon, Calvin hoped that would be over and the two of them would be in prison for life, no longer a worry for them.

With Camico at nine months old and looking more and more like his father every day, she was losing patience and wanted to get out of South America. She knew that if she stayed, once Camico was of age, her father would draw her son into his underworld dealings just as he had her brother and she would never have that. She wanted more for her son and it wasn't a life as a drug dealing, gun running underworld lord or one of her father's minions. She had to get out and hoped Calvin and his team were getting close.

Secretly, she felt like she was helping to move things along by sharing some of her father's secrets with authorities, anonymously of course. Some of her actions had helped because her father's anger manifested itself and he would demand to know how some of his secrets got out. He had no idea she was the leak.

As a young girl, she loved her father, but as she got older and wiser, she saw the kind of man he was and she didn't want to claim him. She tolerated him and her brother because she had to, but one day, she'll have her life with Calvin and Camico and will be able to put this life behind her.

"Sis? You in there?" she heard Valentino say from the hallway outside of Camico's room.

After putting him in his crib, she sat down in the rocking chair in the corner of his room and began to reminisce about her times with Calvin, the only thing that kept her sane.

"Yes," she whispered. "Keep it down because I just got Camico to sleep," he said as he entered the room.

"No problem. Can you step out and talk for a minute? I have to head over to the other house and get back here for a meeting with Pop in an hour. I'm hoping to talk to you right quick," Valentino said.

At one time, he and Sofia had been close, but they drifted in their relationship over the years. As he moved further into his father's world, his world that included her got smaller and smaller because he was home less and less as time went by. His father had trusted him with more each time he succeeded in a task assigned to him. He loved the adrenaline rush and the respect he received when people found out he was the son of Valencio Ramirez. His father was feared and hated, but the name bought respect and now he had it, too. One day, he'd take over his father's illegal operations and make it even bigger than it was.

"Sure," she said, standing and checking to be sure Camico was covered up and had his favorite teddy bear in arms reach in case he woke up. She then followed her brother out of the bedroom and into the hallway.

"What's the deal with this guy who got you pregnant? Pop is trying everything in his power to find this guy to look him in the eye and ask him about getting you pregnant and walking away. You seem to be okay with it, but Pop and I aren't. We don't like it at all," he said.

"You don't have to like it. I'm not a child and I can make decisions in my own life. I don't need you and Pop to buy into what I decide to do with my body or my life. I don't understand why you won't let this go. I'm doing fine raising Camico and his father is an insignificant factor," she lied.

Only she knew about the love between her and Calvin and that was something she wanted to keep to herself. Her brother and father were horrible men and she never wanted Camico to see life with them and experience what she'd experienced for most of her life.

"Is he married or perhaps a member of a rival family? You can tell me and I promise I won't tell Pop," Valentino said.

Sofia didn't believe a word of it.

"You're lying and like I said, there is nothing to tell. I know you would run right from here straight to Poppy and tell him everything. I told you already and I don't want to keep repeating it. He was someone I met and it was over before it started. My blessing from that was Camico and that's all that matters," she explained impatiently.

Valentino leaned closer as she stepped back from him. He was as menacing as her father.

"Unlike Pop who may buy this, I don't. You're lying and keeping something from us. It's only a matter of time before I find out and then he'll know. You need to tell us if there is something we need to know about this situation," he said.

"There is no situation. Now, I want to try and get a nap in while Camico is napping so that I can be wide awake when he wakes up. You can believe whatever you want. There's nothing there. Isn't there a gun you need to purchase, some drugs you need to smuggle or a life you need to take someplace else?" she said snidely.

Sofia spit the words out to him like venom from a snake. They were harsh and deadly. She never minced words when it came to the things her brother and father did. She hated it and wanted nothing to do with it. They may intimidate others, but she didn't fall for it. She was her own woman and preferred that they stay out of her business.

"That's my cue to leave. One day that mouth will work against you and you'll regret speaking against the family business," Valentino said.

"Only when I'm dead," Sofia said and turned to walk back into Camico's room which was connected to hers. She was done talking.

CHAPTER SEVEN

"Today, is the day fellas."

Calvin listened to his commander who gave them instructions on the plan to finally take down Valencio Ramirez. He was ready to get the job done, but he knew there was a secret that no one else knew except Mason. His girlfriend and son were in the house that his team would be raiding. Their lives were at risk and he needed to do something to get them out. He needed to get a message to her as soon as possible. Now was the time for her and Camico to make their exit from the compound where they lived. For the past month, he'd heard nothing from her and was growing more concerned with each passing day.

The last communication from her had come from Camico's nanny. The nanny had somehow connected with Antonia who was able to get him a message that he needed to get Camico out of the house. She felt like something major was happening and she feared for his safety. She had written out a plan of how the nanny would get Camico to him and as soon as she could get away, she would join now that they had Camico's passport. She also had hers and was ready to put this life behind her.

Once he received the message from Sofia, his worry grew ten-fold. Her plan worked against what was the plan of the military to raid the complex and there was a risk she and Camico wouldn't survive. He had to do something and turned to speak to Mason while they listened.

"Mason, I have a problem. Camico and Sofia are in that house right now. If we raid it with them in it, one or both of them could get hurt. I have to say something," he said.

"If you say something, it could blow all of this to hell and you know that, right? You compromised the mission by getting involved with her and then to have a baby with her? Now you want to come clean to the powers that be in order to protect their lives. Are you sure they're actually at the house? You said you haven't heard from her in a month," Mason said.

"She has a few friends that we use to communicate, Antonia and Pierre. There is also a nanny who looks after Camico and a husband and wife who work at a local restaurant that she's good friends with. At one time or another, one of them would get a message to me from her. I was stopped through the restaurant yesterday to see if she's left a message for me and Antonia was there with a note from her. She's planning to get Camico out tonight by way of the nanny. The plan is to get Camico to me and then she would find a way to get out. She doesn't know we're raiding tonight. I need to talk to the commander and come clean. It may be the only way to protect my family and Camico and Sofia are my family," he said.

Calvin was more worried than he was relaying to Mason. The last time he'd heard from Sofia, she was growing leerier of her father and his activities. She felt that he was getting close to finding out that she was the leak he'd been trying to track down. Before he found out, she needed to get Camico out of the house. They discussed a plan, but never got around to talking over the details of how to carry it out.

"I know you love Sofia and Camico is your world, but you knew the risks of getting involved with her. She's his daughter and he holds everyone close to him like they are his possessions. That means Sofia and Camico even if you don't want to admit it. We are about to help the South American people capture Valencio and his entire posse and we can't have any hesitation on your part, even though I know there won't be. I'm just venting here. Anything I can do to help, let me know. I want to help you and I want this mission to go as planned. Let me know what you need from me and I'm on it. Talking to the commander may be a good idea," Mason said.

Calvin listened as his commander ended the meeting and he walked up to him.

"Sir, can I get a minute of your time in private?" he asked.

When he said yes, Calvin followed him into a side room and closed the door. It was now do or die time, he thought.

~~

Sofia paced in her bedroom waiting for the nannies to show up. Her life had become tense over the past few days. Her father had gotten wind of a plan to invade the compound and that details of all of the hiding places in the house had been shared outside of his circle. He was sure no one on his team had divulged the information, but with the growing distance between the two of them, he had begun to suspect her. She had hoped to be gone before he figured it out. If not, there was no way he would ever let her leave and take Camico with her.

She heard a sound and turned toward her bedroom door as it opened.

"Miss Sofia?" Carmen asked.

"Yes, come on in Carmen. Any news yet?" she asked.

"I have a note for you from your gentleman," she said and handed it to her.

Sofia's hands shook as she opened up and read the note:

'Hey, baby. I love you and I love Camico. I'm going stir-crazy not knowing what's going on in that house. The last we spoke, you were afraid, yet you couldn't leave the house. Have you found a

way out yet? I know you plan to get Camico to me, but what about you? I won't survive if anything happened to you. We need to find a way to meet so that I can tell you everything that's going on. We need to get you out. Baby, please get out and do it today if you can."

Sofia knew it was time.

"When did you get this note?" she asked.

"Mister Pierre gave it to my husband this morning. He said he had it for a while, but couldn't get it to my husband until today. I'm sorry it took so long, Missy, but your father is watching everyone closely," Carmen said.

"I know and it's alright. I need to get Camico out of here and it has to be tonight. My father has been suspicious all day and tonight, there are a lot of men here at the house. Something is about to happen. It's time to get Camico through the jungle to safety to his father. We talked about this and you know what to do."

"Missy, you too?" Carmen asked, using the name she called Sofia.

Sofia knew she was asking if she was leaving with Camico.

"I hope so, but if not, you and Andrea need to get Camico to his father. If I'm able to get him out of here, I need you to take him to a place only his father knows about and he'll be safe. I won't be able to leave the house with him, but if my father thinks Camico is still here with me, he won't suspect that

I've had him smuggled out. My only concern is getting my son out of this house. I can take care of myself. I'll make it out. I'm going to write a note for Andrea to take back to Pierre. He'll know how to reach Camico's father," she said.

After Carmen shook her head yes, Sofia took out a pen and paper and scrawled a note to Calvin. In case she didn't make it out, she wanted him to know how much she loved him and that she wanted him to get Camico out of the country and back to the United States, far away from the life in Colombia. She'd never shared with her father who Calvin was and if he could get Camico out, there would be no way for her father to find him if he looked. She promised him she would find a way out, but her priority was getting their son to safety first. She would take too big of a risk leaving with him, but she had a plan. She scribbled out the plan as fast as she could and handed the note to Carmen to hand over to Andrea.

"What next?" Carmen asked.

"Tonight, when I put Camico to bed, come get him. He's been up from his nap for a few hours and will be ready for bed soon. I'm going to put a doll in place of Camico in his crib and I'm hoping that will convince my father that he's still here. It's best to come then because there will be less of a chance that he'll be crying. Take him across the river to the other side of the burned-out cabin and either Camico's father or someone he will send will be there. Even when I don't show up, he goes to that place every night in hopes that I can get away to see him. If he's not there, take him to the restaurant and say the word starlight to Pierre. He will know what to do. That's all you need to know. You know what Camico's father looks like so if you see him, you know you're safe. If there is any danger, you take my son and run like hell into the brush and don't stop until you're safe. Under no circumstances is my father or brother to get their hands on him. Do you understand?" Sofia asked.

"Yes, Missy. I understand. What about you?" she asked.

"I don't know about me yet. As long as I can hold up the ruse that Camico is still here, I will be fine."

Sofia went to her closet and pulled out a duffle bag.

"I worry about you, missy," Carmen said.

"I know and thank you for keeping my secrets and always taking care of Camico. Take this bag and hide it someplace outside of the compound where you can find it. There are things in here for Camico, letters to his father and money for you and Andrea. Once you're away from here, don't look back. My father will know that you helped me and he'll come looking for you. Get as far away as you can and don't come back, ever. There is enough money here for you to start a new life. For now, hide this. Remember, you'll have Camico in your arms tomorrow night and until you get outside of the compound, I don't want anything weighing you down from getting away. Like I said, don't stop. If you have to take Camico with you to get away, you do that only if you can't connect with his father. Camico's life will be in your hands and I'm counting on you. Tell Andrea about this and make sure she gets that note to Pierre today. He will need to get it to Calvin as soon as possible. By morning, my father will know Camico isn't here and if I can't get out, this place is going to be hell. Understand?" she asked.

"Yes, Missy. I will see you tonight after I hide this bag. You can trust that I won't let anything happen to that baby. I love him like he is my own. If I don't get him to mister Calvin tomorrow, I will take him with me and contact Pierre when it's safe to do so. How will I reach you when you leave the compound?" Carmen asked.

"You won't. If I am able to get out of here, Calvin will know where to find me. He'll know what to do. As long as you get Camico to him, don't worry about me. I'll be fine as long as I can get away. If I don't, I wasn't meant to, but at least my son will be away from here. My father can't get his hands on my son or his life will be like my brother's and I can't have that," she said with worry.

"Yes. We don't want that sweet baby turning into another Valentino. Your brother is disturbed," Carmen said.

For the first time in a long time, Sofia smiled.

She understood.

"Yes, he is and that's why it's important to get Camico away from here. Security is familiar with you coming and going and they would never suspect I would let Camico out of my sight, so I know you'll be fine. Go out through the kitchen like you normally would. Don't stray from your usual routine. You always have a big bag with you, so line it with some soft towels and a blanket and put Camico in it. If you move fast, you should be able to get away before anyone knows he's gone. Now, get going," Sofia said, ushering Carmen out of her room.

She was just about to close her bedroom door when her father walked around the corner into her wing of the house.

"Sofia, I'd like to talk to you if you have a minute," he said.

She had to act normal. Plastering a fake smile on her face, she turned toward him as Carmen walked in the opposite direction.

"Sure, Poppy," she said.

"Is Carmen leaving for the day?" he asked.

"No, she came up to see if I needed her to look after Camico if I was going out today."

"You're not going out today. I told you, it's not safe right now for you to be out. Stay in the house," he demanded.

"I'm not going to be a prisoner in this house. Whatever you and Valentino are involved in doesn't involve me," she said defiantly as she walked back into her bedroom and sat at the chair in front of her desk.

"When did you get so insolent and disrespectful?" Valencio asked. "Don't think that because I haven't said anything to counter your attitude, doesn't mean I haven't noticed it and I'm tired of it. I've done nothing but provided for you your entire life and I will have respect from you whether you like what I do or not. It puts a roof over your head, feeds and clothes you and your son. Don't stick your nose up at it. Like I said, I don't want you leaving this house and I mean it. I don't want to have to do anything drastic to make sure you don't leave. I advise you to not test my patience with you," Valencio declared.

Sofia knew she didn't need any trouble and she wanted her father to go away in order for her to finish planning out an escape for her and Camico. She had to get away.

"I'm sorry, Poppy. I think my hormones are out of whack. I may need to go see my doctor tomorrow or the day after to see if she can give me something to tone it down," she said, lying and hoping he would fall for it. That could be her way out of the house.

"No need. I'll have her come see you at the house. You don't need to leave out. When I said stay put, I meant it. I'm going to go see my grandson and then I have some work to do. I trust you'll entertain yourself for the rest of the evening. Do not leave this house!" Valencio demanded before leaving her room.

Sofia plopped down on her bed and watched her father walk through the doorway to Camico's room where he was playing.

"Get a good look at him," she said to herself. "After tonight, you will never see him again."

CHAPTER EIGHT

Calvin waved the two women toward him through the darkness of the high brush and full leaved trees. He had minutes before someone would discover he'd disappeared from the path, but at the moment, his only concern was for his son and Sofia. He took a chance on going to the place where they would meet under the cover of darkness away from her father and brother's prying eyes. He waited as long as he could and was about to turn back to go back to the team who were preparing for tonight's raid on Valencio's compound.

He raised his weapon as the high brush rustled and two women emerged in the dark. He recognized one of them as Camico's nanny and rushed to them. As they got closer, he would see one of them had his son sleeping in her arms. He let out a silent thank you that he was safe. They looked around obviously terrified at being caught in the dead of night with the baby. The situation was tense enough without the possibility of repercussions due to them whisking the baby away from his tyrant grandfather. He looked beyond them in hopes that

Sofia had made it out, too, but saw no sign of her.

"What happened to Sofia? I thought she was going to try and come with Camico," he said.

Carmen handed the baby over to him as they knelt in the darkened field only lit by the half-moon in the sky.

"Mr. Calvin, she couldn't get away. El senor Valencio stopped her from leaving the house earlier today. Tonight, before I left with Camico, he approached her about being some kind of leak or something. I couldn't hear the entire conversation, but he was angrier than I've ever seen him," Carmen said. "I'm afraid for her."

"He wouldn't hurt her," Calvin said.

"He killed Ms. Valentina in cold blood because she betrayed him. That's how he deals with anyone who schemes against him," Carmen said.

"Does he know Camico is gone?" he asked.

"No. Miss Sofia put a doll in his place in the crib. Eventually, he will find out, but she knew it would be long after we left with the baby."

Calvin was terrified. If Valencio found out, he would know for sure that Carmen knew about the raid on the compound, thereby, sealing her fate. He had to get her out, but first he needed to get back to his team. In one hours, they were breaching the barriers and going in search of Valencio and Valentino. He hoped Sofia would make it out and he still had hope that she would find a way. For now, he would do as she always asked and make sure Camico was safe. He pulled a piece of paper out of his pocket.

"Go with the baby to this address and stay there. They will hide you. If you don't hear from me by the end of the day tomorrow, take the baby to Pierre and he will make contact with someone who will get Camico out of the country and to my family in the United States. Whatever you do, don't let him out of your sight."

Calvin looked down at his sleeping son who squirmed in his arms and then calmed down, falling back into a deep sleep.

"We will protect the baby. We won't let anything happen to him," Andrea said.

"Get going and don't look back. Stay put until tomorrow around this time. Everything will be over and either me or Sofia will come for him. Again, if not, read the note and there are instructions in there," he said.

"We're afraid for missy Sofia," Andrea said.

"I can give the baby to Andrea and I can go back for her," Carmen said.

"You know you can't go back. If you return to the house, he'll know you took the baby and you'll be tortured and killed even if you gave up the information that I have him."

"Yes, we know. Do what you can to get missy Sofia out of there."

"That's my plan," Calvin said.

"She told us to tell you two more things. She said

to tell you she loves you very much and second, to look after Camico and never let her father or brother get their hands on him," Carmen said.

Calvin didn't like the sound of that. To him it sounded like Sofia wasn't planning on leaving the compound, at least not alive.

"Those sound like parting words," he said as the two women looked back and forth at each other.

"Senor Valencio doesn't leave loose ends, not even when it comes to his children. Senor Valencio doesn't like deceit and he has his children around as pawns. He's never loved any of them except for Valentino who is a younger version of him and he's just like his father."

"Guard my son's life," he told them before turning around and hustling back through the brush to rejoin his team. They were rounding up at an assigned point and he had thirty minutes to get there. After that, his absence would be noticeable.

~~

The sounds of gunfire rang out through the house and Sofia tried to make a run for the back of the house when she encountered her father and brother in the long hallway.

"What did you do, Sofia? Who did you tell? I know it was you and you don't need to deny it. I received word tonight that my house was going to be raided, but that only came down about ten minutes ago, too late to do anything about it. What have you done? My contact also told me that you were the one working with authorities to turn me in. Are you out of your mind? We're family," Valencio said coming up to her and shaking her like a rag doll. Defiant as ever, Sofia shook free from his grasp.

"I told everyone!" she shouted. "I would do it again if it meant I could get myself and Camico away from you," she added.

"You're not taking my grandson anywhere and you're not leaving either. Don't you know what happens to people who go against me? It's not pretty and there are no loyalties when it comes to traitors. Because of this, you will never see Camico again. I'm going to take him and Valentino and I are getting out of here. I don't care what happens to you, but my grandson is mine. Oh, as far as his American father, I don't know much about him, but I know is name isn't Leo and he has something to do with this raid on my house. You have brought the devil here!" he shouted.

They turned as they heard gunfire getting closer to them.

"I didn't bring the devil here because the devil has lived here my entire life," she shouted. "You will never, ever get your hands on Camico even if that means my life."

Valencio laughed.

"How do you plan on getting him out of this house without the possibility of him getting shot. I'm the only one who knows a way out of here undetected. Valentino, get Camico from his crib and if your sister tries to stop either one of us, shoot her," Valencio said in an ominous voice.

Valentino ran into Camico's room and Sofia smiled with a sinister smirk on her face. Valencio saw it and looked into the bedroom as Valentino turned around looking shocked.

"He's not here!" he shouted.

"What?" Valencio questioned.

"He's not here, Poppy. It's a doll. The baby is gone," he said.

Valencio turned his rage on his daughter and slapped her so hard, she hit the floor like a large weight.

"Where is my grandson?" he demanded. "What have you done with him?"

Sofia wiped her mouth as the back of her hand turned red from the blood gushing from her mouth where her father had slapped her.

"He's gone," she said as she attempted to stand. "I meant it when I said you will never see him again. I sent him to his father."

As gunfire and footsteps got closer, Valencio grabbed her from the floor and dragged her along with him, followed by Valentino.

"Security will only hold them off for so long. We need to get out of here, Pop," Valentino said as they rushed about.

"Back stairwell. I'll hold on to your sister while you lead the way," Valencio said.

As they made their way down the stairs, Valencio saw members of the local police force rushing up the stairs to them.

Sofia couldn't react. Her father had a death grip on her arm and as hard as she struggled to break free, he held on tighter.

"Give it up, Valencio. There is no way you're getting out of here. You and your family need to come with us before we have to use force," a voice called out.

"Come and get me!" he shouted before footsteps raced up the stairs. He reached for his own gun when he saw two officers prepare to shoot. At the last minute, just as gunfire rang out at them, he pulled Sofia in front of him and he held her in place as her body took the bullets that were meant for him. As her body went limp, he threw her at the men as he and Valentino ran back up the stairs to a second secret path out of the house.

They ran for their lives through room after room which was more like a large maze. Someone would have to know the entire layout of the house to find them. Just as they reached the lower landing that would take them out of back of the house through a secret passageway, they encountered two men in military gear that appeared to be from the United States.

"Valencio Ramirez, you're under arrest," Calvin shouted as he got closer.

"You have no jurisdiction here," Valencio

shouted. "I see your United States patch. Get off of my property because my son and I are getting out of here," he said.

"Where's Sofia?" Calvin asked. Peering out, he looked around a large pillar and couldn't get his eyes on Valencio. He knew he was close, but wasn't sure how close.

"I'm going to go around to the back," Mason said in the microphone that connected to Calvin's headset. "Draw them out," he added.

"Sofia? Why?" Valencio asked.

"Where is she? What have you done to her?" Calvin asked. As he made his way through the twists and turns of the house, he tried calling out to her and didn't get a response. He hoped it was because she had found a way out and would be waiting for him at the rendezvous point.

"It's you? You're the one she's been communicating with? Well, have at her. I don't tolerate traitors in my circle and that's exactly what she was," Valencio said. He couldn't see the face of the soldier since it was completely covered.

"What did you do with her? Did you hurt her? She's Camico's mother you monster! What did you do?" Calvin said in anger.

"Camico? How do you know about him?"

"I have him. If you want to see him again, you'll tell me where Sofia is," he said.

"You have him? Who are you? Wait, you're the American. Are you her American lover? Are you

Camico's father? She said she sent the baby to his father. She's been feeding information to the military all this time in pillow talk?" he shouted and laughed.

"Yes, I am Camico's father and either tell me where she is or he'll be gone forever," Calvin said.

"I'm in place," Mason said. "I can see them on the other side of the wall ahead. Let's ice this fool and end this whole thing," he said.

"Last warning, Valencio. Any last words?" Calvin asked.

"Yes, I have a last word for you. I may not see Camico again, but you'll never see Sofia again. She's at the bottom of the staircase with about a dozen bullets in her body."

Hearing that, Calvin lost it. He unloaded his weapon on the wall where Mason said Valencio and Valentino were hiding and he could hear Mason do the same. After a few seconds, he heard a loud thud and knew a body had fallen to the floor. Taking his chance, he rushed around the wall and looked down to see Valentino's bloody body lying on the floor with his eyes opened, clearly dead. Before he could gather his thoughts and look around for Valencio, his body was pierced with several bullets to his legs and his arms before he fell away in the opposite direction of the gunfire.

"Cal!" Mason shouted and rushed toward him. He was able to get a few shots off and possibly two of them went into Valencio before he disappeared behind a passageway. No longer caring, his priority was to get Calvin out of the house.

"Man down," he shouted into his headset alerting the rest of the team. He told them where he thought Valencio had disappeared to and tended to Calvin.

"Get my son," Calvin said. "Get Camico out of here and to Cade," he added right before he passed out.

~~

"Mason," Calvin whispered as he was rushed through the darkened woods to medical care and treatment.

"I'm here. Your SEAL brothers are here with you!" Mason shouted as they continued moving quickly, carrying Calvin, trying not to injure him even more.

"My son. Get my son out of this country and to the United States. You remember what I told you about where Camico is? Go get him by tomorrow night or reach out to Pierre and he will get you to Camico. Use my satellite phone and call my brother. When you do, there is a special code you'll need to use so that he knows it's an emergency. I don't care what happens to me, but get my son out of here before Valencio sends men after him. He killed Sofia, that bastard. Valentino is dead, too. What happened to Valencio?" he asked.

"We don't know. There were so many passageways in and out of that place, he must have gotten out through one and had help. So far, we haven't found him, but don't you worry about that. They did find Sofia's body and I'm sorry, but she's gone, Cal," Mason said.

Hearing his friend say the words took the breath out of him. How could any man kill his own daughter? He thought about her and how much he will miss her and he cried. Camico was going to be motherless and the pain he was feeling, he wasn't sure he would have his father much longer either.

"Get my son, Mason. Get him! If he gets his hands on my son, I'll never see him again. Call Cade and do whatever you can to get him on American soil."

Calvin recoiled when sharp, unbearable pain shot through his body. Things around him seemed to be visually in a tunnel as he struggled to keep his eyes open. No longer able to stand the pain, he succumbed to the darkness that called out to him. His last thought was that he'd lost Sofia.

Mason felt Calvin's body go limp and prayed they would get him to safety before it was too late. He was bleeding heavily from two shots to the thigh and one to his lower leg which appeared to have shattered the bone. He would get him to safety and then do what his friend asked. He would get Camico on American soil or he would die trying.

"I'm already on it, my friend. Camico will be looked after and protected by us, Cal. You have my promise that nothing will happen to him and I'm going to call Cade right away. I need to make plans to get Camico out of here first. I know Valencio will have men all over the place keeping an eye out for him. Trust me when I tell you I will protect your son with my life," Mason said and continued running to safety while praying that is friend would survive.

CHAPTER NINE
Present Day

Callie moved around her parent's house nervously waiting for any word from Cade on Calvin's condition and to also hear where the baby was. As soon as she arrived in Texas and alerted her parents to what was happening, they had already increased security around the ranch even though they weren't expecting any problems. All she knew was Calvin had been injured during a secret mission and he had a son that would soon join her at the ranch. The only warning she'd received which made her father increase security came from Mason, Calvin's friend and that was that the baby was in the middle of a tug of war and could possibly be in danger. She didn't know what that meant, but her father went into protective mode while Cade was away.

After the rocky road she and Cade went through to finally be together, her father considered not only Cade as his family, but also Calvin and their brother Cameron.

After she and Cade decided to make Texas their home-base, they had built their own house on land her father had given them as a wedding gift. Not long after, to keep the family together, Calvin purchased land and began building his own house in Texas. Cameron, though in Florida finishing up his college degree, wanted his own place to stay in when he visited Texas and rather than buy or build a house, Cade secured a condo for him.

Calvin hadn't spent any time at his home which wasn't quite finished yet, but Cameron visited often. With her and Cade going between Texas and California, they always considered their home in Texas their get away from the world, place to go.

Now that Cade and his family needed them more than ever, Callie didn't hesitate to reach out to her parents for help when she knew she needed to focus on Camico, Calvin's son while Cade and his family focused on Calvin.

Callie paced back and forth in the living room of her parent's sprawling complex. She impatiently waited for two phone calls – one from Cade on how Calvin was doing and the other from Mason who would call her the minute Camico was in the country. The minute she got that call, her first priority was getting to him. It saddened her to know that a baby that small had lost his mother and his father was possibly clinging to life. Camico needed to be with family and for now, that would be her and her family.

"Any word from Cade yet?" her mother asked entering the room.

"No, nothing yet. Were you able to reach their grandparents?" Callie asked.

Her mother had volunteered to reach out to Cade's grandparents. As soon as possible, he wanted them on a plane to Calvin. His wounds were severe and he knew their grandparents would want to be there.

"I did and they are on their way to the hospital. The jet landed about an hour ago in Minnesota and Cade had a car waiting for them to immediately get them to Mayo Clinic where Calvin is being treated. Do they know about the baby?" she asked.

Callie had a feeling no one knew about the baby, though she didn't know why Calvin would keep that kind of information from Cade. She knew that the three brothers were close after a rough childhood which improved once they went to live with their grandparents. They had a tight bond and she knew that some kind of extenuating circumstance was the only reason Calvin kept Camico's existence a secret.

"I don't think so. Cade didn't even know. Calvin kept that as a well-guarded secret. If they knew, they didn't mention anything about him," Callie said.

"What do you know about the baby? Was he injured in any way?" her mother asked.

"Well, his name is Camico, he's nine months old and his mother was killed in some sort of altercation in South America. Somewhere in the midst of all that has happened, Calvin is his father.

I don't know how he, as a Navy SEAL got mixed up with the daughter of one of the world's biggest drug lords, but he did and somehow, she was killed and so was her brother and several other men. From what Cade mentioned to me, the father who is responsible for all the carnage, was able to escape. That was all he was able to get from Mason or that was all he shared with me."

Her cell phone beeped as they talked. As soon a she saw Cade's name, she answered and without saying anything, she listened while he updated her. They didn't speak long since he wanted to get back to Calvin. She hung up and turned back to her mother.

"That was Cade. He's staying in Minnesota with Calvin until he's better and the baby's plane is landing right now, here in Texas. He wants me at the airport to pick him up," she said.

Callie rushed around and called for a car to pick her up immediately. Cade had increased his security team after they got married and once he headed to Minnesota, he put his security team on standby at the house to drive her wherever she needed to go.

"What can your father and I do to help?" her mother asked following her around as she gathered her purse, making sure she had all she needed.

Callie turned to her before heading out of the door.

"Pray that Calvin pulls through. This little boy is

going to need his father and I don't think Cade will survive if Calvin doesn't make it. Stay in contact with his grandparents and find out when they are planning to come to Texas after they leave Minnesota. I'm sure the minute they find out about the baby and Calvin is better, they'll want to see him."

"I'll be sure one of the guest rooms is prepared for them or do you want them to stay at your house?" her mother asked.

"I'm going to stay here with you and dad where I will have help looking after Camico. I called Kristine and she's already on her way here, too."

Callie was thankful for her sister. After getting married, she and her husband lived only a few miles away. The minute she called Kristine with news of what was going on, she said she was heading to the house within the hour.

"I'll call Kristine and have her pick up some things a nine-month old would need. I can have some bigger items ordered and delivered within the hour like a crib and other bedroom furniture. I'll have another of the guest rooms prepared for the baby. I'll put him in the one across the hall from the room where you stay when Cade is out of town on business."

Callie hugged her mother tight as they saw lights shine through the large bay living room windows, no doubt her driver.

"You're the best, mom. I can't thank you enough

for all that you're doing to help," she said.

"Nonsense. Cade and his family are just as much a family to your father and I as you and your sister are. Call me if you need anything else. I'll let your father know you're leaving. He's out with his men locking the property down. I don't know what happened with Calvin, but if his friend said we need to protect Camico with our lives, your father is already on top of that. You go get the baby and bring him back here. Once the baby is here, no one will be allowed on the ranch that hasn't cleared with your father."

"Thanks for helping, Mom," Callie said.

"To think, we were just getting prepared for your pregnancy and we knew we had about five more months to get ready for that and now with Camico arriving, we need to be ready now with a crib, formula, clothes and everything else he will need. How are you feeling? Be mindful that you're pregnant and you need to take it easy, too."

"I will, mom and I'm feeling good. I just want to get Camico to safety and get that weight off of Cade's mind. He needs to focus on Calvin."

"Good. I have things under control here. Get going so that you can get back here."

Callie shook her head and rushed out to the car. The minute she was seated in the back, she received a text from Mason of where she needed to go when she got to the airport. She reached down and touched her own swelling belly where their growing baby was nesting quietly. She had Cade had only a few months to focus on her pregnancy once she'd found out and now their lives had an additional priority which was getting Calvin the best care possible and getting Camico in her arms.

She typed back her reply to Mason to let him know that she was on her way. She was happy to see that a car seat had already been installed in the back of the stretch black Navigator truck that pulled up to take her to the airport. She said a silent pray for Calvin, Cade and Cameron. Calvin had to pull through if they were all going to survive this. Right now, she had a job to do and that was to protect Camico. She didn't know who or what she was protecting him from, but Cade counted on her and Camico's life was in her hands. She thought she had some months before she'd have to buckle down to care for a baby, her own, but with Camico coming, she needed to be ready soon, which meant right now. Somewhere out there in the world, there was a threat to Camico and her family wouldn't let anything happen to him.

~~

Valencio emerged from the wooded jungle and found respite with friends. He didn't know how long he'd been running, but between trying his hardest to get far away and to stay off of anyone's radar, he finally reached a place where he felt safe. As far as he could tell, two days had passed and by now, the authorities knew he wasn't anywhere on the compound or at any of his other houses. Running, he had to find a place where no one would look for him and he could lay low as he healed.

As the house appeared on the horizon, he stooped down low to see if there was any movement. He had grown up in the overgrown fields that made up Colombia and no one knew the lay of the land better than him.

Over the year's he'd built many escape routes and had bought enough people's silence that he was sure that as long as he could get to the house that he could now see, he would be safe. The biggest issue was the wounds he did his best tending to until he could get better care. From what he could assess, he took a bullet in the hip, one in the side and one in his leg, that didn't seem too bad. It was the one in his side that had caused him to pass out twice while on the run.

Checking out the house again, he saw several people come and go and one of those people was Horatio, one of his top security men whose job it was to stay close to the pulse of Colombia, letting him know of any word about him on the street. Horatio hadn't been at the house during the raid, but he knew that all of the men who had been there were now dead. He needed to regroup and fast.

Horatio was getting in his car and driving away from the property. Valencio knew he needed to wait until the cover of darkness in order to reach the house. The land between him and the house was flat and the grass had recently been cut. The only trees for cover were behind the house and there was a large wall he'd have to scale to get around that side. His best bet would be to wait it out until he saw Horatio return and until nighttime fell.

Turning around, he rushed back hide in a bunch of trees he'd passed, hoping it would provide cover until later. Reaching them, he huddled in the mass and hunkered down trying to focus on anything except the excruciating pain from his injuries. What kept him fueled was the revenge he knew he needed to seek for the death of his son, daughter and his men. He now knew that the man Sofia had kept a secret was United States military and though he never got the chance to see his face, he had connections and would find him. When he did, he would get his grandson back and kill the man who entered is daughter's life and wreaked havoc on his.

Valencio couldn't shake the fact that Valentino was dead, Sofia was gone and his only grandson was gone. He was alone, except for his grandson. All he could feel is rage.

He smiled through the pain in his side knowing that he would do anything to get his grandson back. It's time for those in the United States that he paid millions, to help him get his revenge by finding out who the mystery soldier was.

CHAPTER TEN
Two Months Later

"How is my brother, doc?" Cade asked. He and Cameron hadn't left Calvin's side since the moment they'd arrived at the hospital after Calvin was brought back to the United States from Colombia where all hell had broken out and Calvin had been injured.

After getting the call from Mason, Calvin's best friend and fellow Navy SEAL team member, he'd hopped on a plane and met Calvin's plane as it landed back in the states at the Mayo Clinic in Minnesota, the top ranked hospital in the country. Through the many connections he had acquired through his career in the entertainment industry, he was able to get Calvin moved to this hospital though he was originally instructed that he would be flown to a military hospital. Cade learned a long time ago just how far his money went and, in this case, he thought only of what Calvin would need and knew that need would be met at Mayo.

"He's coming along a lot better. In the two months that he's been here, he has improved significantly. The fact that he woke up yesterday is a good sign after being in a coma all this time."

"Is there any brain damage we need to be worried about? Two months is a long time to be down," Cade said.

"It is, but we're hopeful about Calvin. He's strong in body and in his will."

"I hear you, but he hasn't woken back up again since yesterday," Cade said with worry.

"He needed that rest now that he's woke. He mentioned his son again yesterday while he was briefly woke. The fact that he remembered he had a son and was able to say his name is a great sign. I wasn't sure what he would remember. His body and his mind need to rest now, so I gave him a sedative to keep him under a little longer. He needs to let his mind and body rest. He recognized you and your brother, his wounds are healing good and his vitals are improving. The only thing we'll need to verify is how well he can move around on his leg. With the bullets we removed from him, that leg gives me concern. I won't know the extent until he's lucid. The sedative should wear off in a few hours and we'll try talking to him again."

Cade exhaled in relief, happy to hear the Calvin was showing signs of improvement. That's a far cry from what he'd seen the moment the aircraft carrier arrived with him on it two months ago.

Other than immediate care given to Calvin when they first placed him on the carrier, nothing else had been done and he looked pretty bad. He had been completely covered in blood though his medical team did their best to clean him up. To see him now knowing he had finally awoke from the coma, he was feeling hopeful that Calvin would be fine.

"This is all good to hear. It's been a long two months of waiting for him to wake up or to give any sign that he was getting better."

"I know you could probably use some sleep. You've been here every day since he arrived."

"I'm good. I can't be anyplace else. My brother, Cameron, just took my grandparents back to the hotel to get some rest and when he gets back, I'm going to go catch up on sleep and check-in with my wife. I'm glad Calvin is coming along good. If you think he'll be awake later today, I'm going to hang around. I want him to see me when he wakes up," Cade said.

He nervously paced thinking of how close they had come to losing Calvin. He had never been more scared in his life hearing that he'd been injured during a mission and was being brought back to the United States. The minute he saw Calvin, he knew it was bad.

"He may wake up, but he'll be in and out," Dr. Bell said.

"Either way, I want to be here. I need him to know we're here. I don't have the full story of what happened to him and when he wakes up, he needs to see family."

"You're a good brother. I know how busy you are and it's good you were able to drop everything to be here for him."

When the doctor extended his hand for a shake, Cade took it and thanked him for giving his brother the best of care.

"There is nothing in this world more important to me than family, especially my brothers."

"Dr. Bell?"

Cade and the doctor turned as a nurse walked up to them.

"Yes?" Dr. Bell said.

"He's waking up."

"Already? I gave him a sedative," Dr. Bell said.

As soon as the words left her mouth, Cade turned and rushed down the hall with the doctor close on his heels. When he entered Calvin's room, a nurse was checking his vitals and he noticed Calvin looking around the room.

"I'm here, Cal," Cade said, going to the head of the bed so that Calvin wouldn't have to move too much to see him.

"Cade?" he heard Calvin say with a gruff voice. He could tell it pained him to try and speak.

"Don't talk if it still hurts."

"I'm fine," Calvin was able to get out.

"Let me get a look at you before you try talking a mile a minute," Dr. Bell said.

Cade stood back and watched as he checked

Calvin's eyes, ears, mouth and moved his arms to check how far he could move them before Calvin winced in pain.

"You're doing good, Cal," Cade said, encouraging him while seeing the strain of the pain look on his face as the doctor checked his dexterity.

"I won't bother with the leg yet since it's in traction anyway. It'll be a few more weeks before we will know what kind of movement he'll have in the leg. We repaired the bones that were shattered and he'll need a lot of physical therapy."

"You know he's a SEAL, doc. Will he be able to go back to that? The military is his life," Cade said. He looked to Cal and saw that same question in his eyes.

"If he follows the regiment I'll prescribe for him when it comes to therapy, I have no doubt he'll be able to get back to being a SEAL. Time will tell and it won't be easy. It's because of the training his body has endured that has allowed him to heal as much as he has and with the way the bullets tore his leg up, it could have been worse, but it wasn't."

"That's good to know."

"I'm going to give you some time alone with him. He shouldn't move too much," Dr. Bell said.

"Gotcha, doc. Thanks for all you've done."

"Thanks for the confidence in sending him here."

"When I asked who the best was, you were on the top of everyone's list and I wanted the best for him. You and your team are the best and my family is grateful."

"Let me know if you need anything and I'll be back around in about an hour to check on him. The nurses know how to reach me if need be before then."

Cade thanked him again and watched as he exited the room. He then turned to Calvin, saying a little prayer in his head that his life had been spared. The military had been tight-lipped as he expected, but he knew whatever Cal could remember, he would tell him the story.

"Hey, bro. Welcome back," Cade said. "You gave us all a scare like you wouldn't believe. Cam is on his way back here. Gram and gramps are here, too. We've been pulling for you."

He watched as Calvin struggled to speak. He'd had a tube for the ventilator down his throat for almost two months and he knew Calvin's throat had to still be pretty raw.

"Where is here?" Calvin was able to get out as he moved his head from side to side trying to focus.

"You're in the hospital at Mayo. Do you remember anything about what happened to you?" he asked.

"Camico? Where is Camico?" Calvin asked.

Cade saw him getting frustrated and anxious as he began making an attempt to get out of the bed.

"Calm down and stay still. I got you and I have Camico. He's fine and in Texas with Callie and her family. She's been looking after him since he arrived in the States two months ago. Mason took good care of him until he was able to get him on U.S. soil, which according to him wasn't easy."

Seeing a tear run down the side of Calvin's face, Cade grabbed the box of tissues and wiped it away.

"Camico," Calvin said again.

"He's perfectly healthy, too. He's a chubby little guy and so happy. Callie said he's doing great and trying to walk. I told her the minute you were awake, I would let her know so that we could get Camico here for you to see for yourself that he's okay. I heard his mother didn't make it. That was a secret you really kept hidden. Why didn't you tell me about her and Camico?" Cade asked.

"I was planning on getting them away from there and here in the States when all hell broke loose," Calvin said, struggling to get his words out. Images of Sofia's beautiful face splayed across his mind and knowing that she was gone was tearing him up inside.

"When you feel up to it, I want to hear everything. For now, I want you to focus on getting better," Cade said.

He watched as Calvin struggled to sit up.

"I have to tell you something," he said and Cade moved closer.

"That's fine, but you have to stay still which means no sitting up. Dr. Bell doesn't want you moving too much. You have internal injuries that need to heel and you have stitches everywhere that we don't want to burst. Tell me what you need, but then no more talking for a while, okay?" Cade asked. Now that he was awake, he didn't want there to be a setback because Calvin couldn't keep still. When Calvin nodded his head, he listened.

"Camico is in danger. There is a lot about this you don't know, but you have to keep him safe. The man who shot me is still alive and I'm not sure if he knows who I am yet, but if he doesn't he'll be coming for my son. He'll do everything in his power to take Camico away. I can't prevent that from here. You said they're in Texas. Are they at my house?" Calvin asked.

Calvin had a house that wasn't quite ready yet. Cade had gotten men on completing the construction assuming Calvin would eventually come back to Texas when he was released.

After coming back to the states for Cade's wedding to Callie, Cade had begun working on his house. Mason was the one who told him that Calvin had built that house and made it as secure as it was because he had been planning to bring Sofia and Camico to the United States to live and he knew he would need to make sure they were safe and at all times. The few times Cade had been there, he thought Calvin was going overboard with all the secret rooms and passageways, but now he knew there was a reason behind it.

Being a Navy SEAL, he saw a lot and being safe was always top on his list. In case of any emergency, Cade knew that he and his family could survive a long time in the house that Calvin was having built, but it wasn't quite finished. Knowing his brother the way he did, a week after arriving in Minnesota, he got the construction company to work on the house and he'd already contacted an interior designer who worked with Callie on various projects who had already started delivery furniture.

"No, they're in Dallas at Callie's parents' house. She's been staying there since she's taking care of Camico and her family is helping with that. According to Mason, we needed to keep Camico safe and the ranch was the best place for that. Trust me when I tell you that Camico is safe. Callie's father's ranch is a place no one would want to venture onto unwelcomed. You know, the house Callie and I built is on that property from land her parents gave us when we got married. Gram and gramps have been there a few times over the past few months that you've been here and you know they are already trying to spoil your son, their first grandchild. Having Camico, you have made her one happy lady. Don't worry because soon, Camico will have a little cousin and Gram, can spoil them together," he said, smiling.

"Callie's pregnant?" Calvin asked.

"She sure is. She's seven months and we're excited. You know she wants a bunch of babies and I plan to give her all the babies she wants. She's getting good practice with Camico. I don't want you to worry about him. Mason connected us with two security teams and I hired both along with the team Callie's father has. Camico is better protected than most military bases. Callie has been talking about you to him and showing him pictures of you so that he will remember who you are. We weren't sure how long you would be here. Trust me when I tell you, no one is getting my nephew."

"Who's after my nephew?" Cameron said coming into the room. "Hey, bro, you're woke?" he said coming up to the bed.

"I'm still here," Calvin stumbled out and attempted to laugh until pain hit him.

"You being here is a good thing. You had me worried there for a bit. You look a lot better than you did when I first got here."

"Trust me when I tell you that I'm lucky to be here," Calvin said.

"How bad was it?" Cameron asked.

"As bad as it could get. Bad enough that I couldn't protect Camico's mother, Sofia. I loved her with everything in me and I couldn't protect her. She died trying to get herself and Camico out of Colombia."

Cade sat in the chair closest to the hospital bed and pulled it as close to the bed as he could get.

"I know this is hard right now. I also know that you had to have loved her deeply because I can hear it in your voice and it's all over your face. There is nothing you can do about that right now. I'm sure she would want you to focus on getting well so that you can take care of the son the two of you made and that's what I want you to do. Cam and I will be here. Get some rest and we'll talk later when you wake up."

Calvin couldn't take his mind off of Sophia and the way she died. Instead, he'd like to focus on how they met. As he drifted back off to sleep, Sofia beautiful face was the last thing he remembered and he hoped his dreams would be filled with how they met and not with how she died or the pain his body was going through. He didn't know how long it would take for him to heal. He just wanted to get to his son.

CHAPTER ELEVEN

Ava Cortez was excited to finally have a few days off from taking on her usual clients as well as new physical therapy patients. Her life had been a whirlwind since the moment she packed up her life in California and moved to Dallas, Texas. Now that she could finally get back to her life without hiding, she needed a change from her life in California though she missed her friend, Mackenzie, once Mackenzie Ellis, now Mackenzie Blackwell.

They met while she had been living under cover and working as a nurse where Mackenzie worked as a doctor. With Mackenzie's help and that of her new husband, Trey and his friends, she and her sister and brother were once again free to come out of the shadows and live full lives.

Her sister, Nina had once dated a bad guy and she had been a witness to a lot of his illegal dealings. One day, she witnessed him kill a man and as the only witness to what happened, the man she thought she loved and who she thought loved her had put out a hit on her life. When he couldn't find her, he knew about Ava and their brother Vinnie and so the three of them had to go underground. It went well until her sister got tired of living that way until the trial and made a mistake. She was located by her ex-boyfriend's men and the effort to save her life and the life of her sister and brother was in the hands of Trey Blackwell and his team of Navy SEAL brothers who together had formed a company called, Game Changers.

They provided reconnaissance and private security and extraction services in touchy situations the United States wanted to stay away from. Through all of that, her sister had fallen in love with one of the men, Dustin, who had been responsible for her rescue and she decided to make her life in California with him.

As much as Ava loved and missed the friendships she'd made, she wanted a fresh start and to get out of nursing and back to her first love, being a physical therapist. Taking money she'd saved up over the years, she connected with an old friend in Texas and they formed their own rehabilitation company and finally after months of planning, she packed up her belongings and moved to Texas.

Finally getting up and walking into the kitchen of her condominium, she was about to prepare breakfast for herself when her cell phone rang. She could hear it, but couldn't find it. She remembered coming home the night before and wanting nothing to do with any electronics. While working, she was glued to her phone and iPad non-stop and she wanted a break from both for the four days respite that she was planning to take.

This was the first time in almost a year that she'd taken any time off. It took months to get the business up and running and now that things were going well and they were constantly booked, she needed some downtime. This break would allow her time to look over the applications of potentials new hires. Thankful for all of the clients they had and were getting on a daily basis, it was time to increase the staff.

Chasing down her ringing phone, she would check to see who was calling, but anything work related, she was planning to ignore for the next several days. She meant it when she said she needed some time to herself.

Finding it, she grabbed it just as it stopped ringing. Seeing the call was from her sister, she began dialing her number back when the phone started ringing again.

"Hey, sis!" she said with excitement.

"I was wondering what was going on when you didn't answer which is unlike you. I'm calling to make sure you were taking the days off that you promised me you were going to take. You work too hard," Nina said.

"Hello to you too and yes, I'm off for the next couple of days. I'm looking forward to relaxing. How are things with you? Is Dustin still treating you well?" she asked.

"Sis, now you know Dustin is the best man in the world. He rescued me, so what more could I ask for. Of course, he's the sexiest man I've ever met and I love him with everything in me. Yes, he's treating me well. What about you? Are you dating anyone yet?"

Ava thought before she responded. Her sister and brother had both been riding her case about her lack of a personal dating life. She admitted that while she lived in California, she was hesitant about getting involved with anyone because she couldn't be honest with anyone about who she really was and the fact that she was hiding out in plain sight. Though she kept her first name, her last name wasn't real and neither was most things she told people about her life. She focused more on work than on having a love life, pretty much how her life continued once she moved to Dallas.

"Why are you so worried about my love life? I'm good," Ava said.

As her sister talked she turned on her Keurig and looked in her cabinet for her favorite latte coffee.

"I want to see you happy and in love. It was my fault that you, Vinnie and I had a few years of our lives taken away because we had to live off the grid for a while. Now that we don't have to do that anymore, I want to be sure both of you are living life to the fullest. I already know Vinnie is now that he has his girlfriend and son back in his life. How's the company coming along?" Nina asked.

Ava knew her sister worried every day that there were no lasting negative feelings about how their lives had changed because of her sister's desire to live the good, fast, expensive life and it almost led to each of their deaths.

"It's coming along great. This is the first time I've had a break in the year since I moved here and we got the company up and running. It feels good to disconnect even if it's only for a few days. When are you coming to visit?"

"I'm hoping to come one day in a few months. Dustin is on a mission and the moment this case is over, he said he wants to take a trip away someplace. I want to come visit you for a few days before we go away if that works for you."

Ava was excited. She had talked to her sister and brother almost daily, but hadn't seen either of them since she left California.

"Yes, that works for me. I'll take a few days off when you get here and show you around."

"I hope by then, they'll be a male friend you can introduce me to. You're the oldest and I expect you to provide me with a niece or nephew in the next few years, so you need to get on that immediately."

"Babies? Girl, you better stop smoking that

stuff!" Ava joked. "I don't think kids are in my future especially since I'm not seeing anyone."

"Well, I know you had reservations about dating before, but that's not the case now so there is no excuse."

"Trust me, as soon as that perfect man finds me, you'll be the first person I tell. For now, let me enjoy my newfound life a little while longer by myself."

"Okay. I'll let it go for now, but I'm going to keep asking you. It's because of me you had to postpone your life and I want to be sure we're all getting back on track."

"Sis, I love you and believe me when I say, my life is fine. I'm not longing for something other than what my life consists of now. I'm getting used to living my life out in the open again and I'm loving it. A relationship is not a priority for me right now and at thirty, I have plenty of time to get married and give you a niece or nephew. I'm good right now, okay?"

"Okay, I hear you. Anyway, I wanted to call and check in on you and to let you know that Trey Blackwell is going to be calling you about a new client, someone he and Dustin knew from the navy. Whoever this person is, it's a close personal friend of his and he doesn't want anyone else working with him, but you. I told him you were off for a few days and he said he would connect with you when you were back to work."

"Tell Trey to call me anytime. He doesn't have to wait until I'm back to work. If he needs my help with anything, I'm available. If it wasn't for him and his team, who knows where we would be today. They saved our lives," Ava said.

"That's what I said. I'll tell Trey to call you sooner. I think the help he's looking at for his friend is sooner rather than later. I hear he's sexy," Nina said. "He has to be, he's a navy SEAL and they're all fine!" she added.

"Don't go there. You know I don't mix business and pleasure."

"Sis, you're not mixing anything with pleasure right now. I'm just saying," Nina laughed.

"I'm hanging up now. I have some things to do and they don't involve you trying to hook me up. Love you and I'll call you later," Ava said and hung up.

Grabbing her cup of coffee, she ventured into her family room and crawled into the corner of her black leather sectional, turned on the television and settled in for a quiet day at home. Her sister's words rang out loud in her head as she tried to focus on finding something on the television that would capture her attention for more than a few minutes.

Leave it to her sister to constantly shine a spotlight on her non-existent dating life. It didn't bother her until her Nina brought the subject up on every phone call or face-time they did weekly. What did it matter that she hadn't been out on a real date in years? Was there something wrong with a woman who hasn't had sex in a few years?

Now that she said the words in her head, she sounded like a woman who lived in a house alone with her forty cats – no social life at all. She wasn't one to really put herself out there that she would like to be involved with someone. She was used to focusing on work and not leaving a lot of time for anything else. She wasn't running from being involved with a man and if the opportunity afforded itself, she looked forward to embracing it.

CHAPTER TWELVE

"I want to go to Texas. I appreciate everything everyone has done for me here at Mayo, but rehabilitation can be done anywhere, including there and there is where my son is," Calvin pleaded.

After spending the last three months at Mayo following his extraction from South America, Calvin was ready to leave and get back to his son who was currently living in Texas with his brother and sister-in-law and her family.

He was happy that he was able to face-time with Camico every day and he was thankful that Callie put her own schedule aside and brought Camico to Minnesota to see him several times over the past three months. Now, he was ready to see his son on a daily basis and he wanted to get back to some kind of normalcy in his routine. Living in a hospital was not helping with that. He knew his family wanted him to stay at Mayo, but he was feeling good enough that he could finish his recovery and care in Texas where he could be closer to family.

His grandparents, who had been in Minnesota with him most of the time, were currently in Texas with Camico where he knew his grandmother was finding it hard to tear herself away from his jolly little son who was now a year old, walking and trying to talk.

Cade had reservations about him being moved from Mayo, but he had been working through what he would say to convince him that the time was now to get him back home. He knew that with Cade's help, his house was now finished and ready for him to move into. He was tired of a hospital being his home.

Calvin watched for any signs of discontent on Cade's face and not seeing any, he felt like he'd made his point. For the past twenty minutes, he'd been trying to convince Cade to move him home for rehabilitation and therapy back in Texas where he could be closer to Camico. He wanted to see his son every day. Callie told him of Camico's struggles in the beginning because he was constantly looking for his mother. He wanted him to know he still had his father. Camico was all he had left of Sofia and he made her a promise that he'd take care of their son and to him, he wasn't doing that those few days a month he got to spend with him. Callie could no longer fly being a month away from delivering her own baby, so he now had to settle for facetiming with him.

"You're right, you can do rehab anywhere, but

you're already here where some of the best doctors in the country are. I'm sure the physical rehab technicians are the best here, too. Haven't the sessions you've had already gone well?" Cade asked.

"They have and I'm feeling much better. I have more movement in this leg than they thought I'd have at this stage. I'm well enough to be moved and I think I can even do it from home. All I need is the necessary equipment brought into my house and I can get a nurse to help out with Camico. I'm sure Camico has been a handful for Callie."

Cade looked at him sideways.

"I know you're not saying Camico has overstayed his welcome at my house because that's far from the truth. Callie has loved looking after him and Gram will probably talk gramps into moving to Texas sometime soon because she spends a lot of time between here and there."

Calvin felt rejuvenated in his effort to convince his brother. Though he knew he didn't need Cade's permission because he could make his own life decisions, Cade was that father figure that he and Cameron needed and he always looked up to him.

"See? If I was home, Gram wouldn't have far to go and if they want to move to Texas, between my house or yours, they would be fine. There's only a little over an hour between our two houses as opposed to them having to fly here. I need to be close to my son, Cade. I know the decision is mine, but I want your support. When are you planning to go back to California? You can't put your career on hold forever?"

"Callie has been asking the same thing, but she's one month away from delivering the baby and I don't want her home with me in California in that rat race. I'm going to be filming a new movie in Texas, so I'll be home for quite a few months with only occasional trips to the west coast."

"See, everyone will be in Texas," Calvin said.

"Alright, if you want to head to Texas, we need to get all of your care lined up, especially the physical therapist."

"I've already gotten a referral for one. Her name is Ava Cortez. I've been told she's the best and she's ex-military, having done four years right out of high school. She's worked with a lot of injured soldiers and right now she's in Texas. Trey and Dustin, you remember them, referred her to me. She was willing to come here to work with me, but since she also lives in Texas, that's a sign that I should be in Texas for convenience. The hospital here will put in a call to her about her availability and to let her know I'm interested in someone coming to the house."

"She?" Cade asked.

"Yeah, she."

"I hope you're nicer to her than I hear you being to the therapists here. You can be Navy SEAL demanding with them and they're probably happy to see you go," Cade joked.

Calvin laughed.

"Not as happy as I will be to leave here. The care has been great, but as time passes, the more I'm concerned for Camico's safety. I know your house and the ranch are great, but I will feel better having Camico around me every day."

"You have one spunky little kid. He's getting big and at a year old, he loves to explore. Make sure you get him some pets. He loves animals. Callie's dad takes him to the barn and it's the cutest thing to see how excited he gets when he sees the farm animals."

"See, I'm missing everything," Calvin said, solemnly.

"Don't even try it. Callie told me she does facetime with you every day so that you don't miss anything."

"You're right, she does and he gets excited when he sees my face on the other side of the screen. I miss him."

"I know you do. You'll be in Texas in a week and you'll wish you were back here. He is a handful and now that he's walking and trying to pull himself up on everything, you have to watch him closely. What about a nurse? Callie has one that comes in and helps her out. I can have her check out a few and have backgrounds done before you get back."

"That'll help. I'm going to ask Gram to come help for a little bit. She and Gramps will love it in Texas. Are you still trying to get them to move closer to us?" Calvin asked.

"Us?" Cade chuckled. "You came home for my wedding, put plans in place to build yourself a house close to mine in Texas and you've literally spent one day in it since you built it."

"I know. Now, it looks like I'll be spending even more time there because of this leg," Calvin said.

"What's the military saying? Are you planning to return to duty? What's the word on the leg being back to normal?" Cade asked.

"Doctors say the leg will eventually heal, but to get it back to the condition it needs to be in for me to get back to my team, that could take up to a year."

"Wow, a year? How are you going to deal with that?"

"Most of that time I'll be dealing with rehab and it shouldn't drive me too crazy being still. Besides, I want to spend as much time with Camico as I can."

"That's one remarkable kid you have. What happens in a year when you decide to go back to join your team? What happens to him then?"

Calvin started to respond and then didn't. He hadn't thought that far ahead. He loved being a SEAL, but the most important thing in his life now and forever would be his son.

"I haven't told you this yet, but the military is giving me to option of a promotion to teaching if I'm not up to going back into the field. I may take them up on that. Now that I have Camico, I'm not sure I can leave him for months at a time for missions where I don't know if I'll ever return from them. It's a lot to think about. He's already lost one parent. I don't want to make it two."

"I'm sorry I didn't get the chance to meet Sofia. She sounds like a lovely girl. In all that's been going on with you, I wasn't able to tell you Callie and Gram had a small memorial service for Sofia at the house with just the family there. We didn't know Sofia, but we wanted to do something."

"Gram mentioned it to me the last time she was here. She said she and Gramps went and how nice it was. I'm grateful to Callie for everything she's done. She didn't have to do any of this," Calvin said.

"No, she didn't, but she's family and this is what family does. We are all here for you to do whatever you need. If you decide to go back, you know Callie and I will take care of Camico. We are his family now and it's best if he's not in an unstable environment."

"I appreciate that and I know he'll be fine with you. I don't know what I'll do yet, but I'll think about it and get back to you once I'm healed," Calvin said.

"I need to fly out to California for a big meeting. Go ahead and work on the plan to get you to Texas and I'll have your house cleaned and aired out. I'll be done in two days and by then, you should have everything worked out? My plan can fly you home to Texas when you're ready," Cade said.

"Great. In the meantime, Trey Blackwell is coming to town to do some additional work on the house, making it more secure."

"I understand about Sofia's father, but do you think he's really going to risk coming into this country to get his grandson back? Does he even know who you are? It's been months and we haven't heard anything. Mason and his men have been scouting out the airwaves for any sign of retaliation from him and they haven't been able to find any sign that you're on his radar. I understand he doesn't actually know your name," Cade said.

"Yeah, Mason told me. I'm just being safe. He made threats that I took to heart. Mason said he's heard that Valencio has been underground since everything happened, but there has been talk that he's putting large dollars out for anyone who can give him information on who I am. He's a rich and powerful man. I know Sofia didn't tell him about me other than I was an American, especially my name. That doesn't mean he won't one day find it. Valencio is a determined and demented man. I wouldn't put it past him to look for Camico for the rest of his life. With the dealings he's had over the years, he has connections in this country that may help him. He blames me for Sofia and his son's death. Mason shot his son, but he blames me for it. Sofia is on him. Any man who could have his own wife killed and use his daughter as a human shield would do anything to get Camico from me because he hates me. I'm not taking any chances."

"I hear you. Let's focus on getting you to Texas and we'll deal with Valencio later. I'll contact this Maxwell guy and get the ball rolling on whatever you want done to the house until you get there."

"How's Cam doing?" Calvin asked.

"He's finishing up his last year of school for his master's degree in Broadcasting and Journalism. He'll have a minor in sports management."

"So, he decided against sports management or anything sports related? I hear he's been approached several times about playing professional ball."

"He's got the bug from me for being in front of the camera. I bought a condo for him in Texas so that when he comes to town, he can have some privacy. The last time he came to town, he stayed with us and Callie woke in the middle of the night to get a middle of the night snack and encountered a naked model in the kitchen, someone Cam brought to the house. The next day, she asked me to either build an addition on to our house for him or talk to him about naked women roaming around her house. He's still apologizing for that every time he calls her to check on his nephew. Instead of adding to the house, he asked for a condo so that he could have privacy. You have no idea the number of women our little brother parades around with," Cade joked.

"Yeah, I heard about the condo, but didn't know

the story behind it. That's wild. He is a chip off the old block, isn't he? You and I haven't always been the best examples when it comes to parading women around in front of him."

"He's not as wild as you and I were, but he's sowing some serious wild oats!" Cade said laughing.

"He got that from you! I told you your lifestyle would one day rub off on him. Maybe now that you're an old married, settled down man, he'll pick up that vibe and not have a different woman in his bed every night."

"Yeah, well now, he can do all his business in his own place. I'm glad you both decided to make Texas your home," Cade said.

"Me, too. I know your work life is based out of Los Angeles, but it's good to see you in your element away from that rat race."

"That's what Callie said. I love that she's close to family when I'm running from coast to coast or country to country. This new movie I'm working on in Texas will have me close by and she's ecstatic about that."

"How's her clothing line coming along?" Calvin asked.

"That's the best part. She can do that from Texas and it's booming. Her sister joined her company and the construction of her new office building complete with a warehouse for her product is just about complete. When you're in Texas and better, I'll take you to see it. I contracted with this firm, out of California to work on the design and construction. They're the ones who built my house and office park in Los Angeles. The owners, Duron Knight, Tyrone Davis and Michael Bailey are the fastest growing architecture firm in the past few years. Their main base is in Atlanta and they now have offices in Los Angeles and Chicago."

"I'm glad to hear things are working out well with you and Callie and that mess that happened that almost broke you up was resolved quickly."

"Yeah, everything was almost ruined when she overheard me say she wasn't important to me. She high-tailed it back to Texas and wouldn't talk to me until I begged her parents to let me see her and explain I did that to protect her image. Now, we're happily married and in a month, our first bundle of joy will be here. Camico will have a cousin to play with," Cade said.

"I love that idea. Our family is the only family he'll have."

"Bro, our family will be enough. When Valencio's compound was seized, there were a lot of Sofia's things in the house. I had them boxed up and sent to your house in Texas. There were pictures, letters and a few journals I thought you might like to keep for Camico."

Calvin could feel tears welling up in his eyes. He missed Sofia and the life they were planning to live together as a family raising their son on American soil. He would never let Camico forget that his mother gave up her life for him.

"Really? I appreciate that. I have a few pictures of Sofia, but that was all."

"I haven't seen anything that was in the boxes, but there were eight of them full of mementos. I'm going to let you get some rest. I have a flight to catch. If you need anything, Cam is flying in over the weekend. Call me if you need me or call Callie. I know the circumstances of you being home are crazy, but I'm glad you'll be around for a while. Know that if you decide to go back to being a SEAL, we will all look after Camico. I love you, Cal," Cade said.

"I love you, too."

Calvin laid back in his hospital bed and thought about all that had taken place. He missed Sofia terribly, but he was glad he had Camico and thankful for family. Every day, Callie found time to face-time with him so that Camico would know who his father was. Every time he saw his little man and those little white teeth poking through his gums when he smiled, his heart melted. There was a lot of his mother in him, a mother who would have his love forever.

Regret began to set in when he thought of a different scenario that would have saved Sofia. He knew her father was ruthless, but to use his own children the way he had was callous and cruel. He would do what Sofia asked and take care of their son. Reaching for his phone, he put in a call to Trey

Maxwell at Game Changers in California. In order for him to take care of his son, he needed to secure the home where they were going to live. Soon, he would be in Texas and it was time he made plans for the care he would need and the security he would have on call around the clock. First, he needed to get more information about the physical therapist that Trey was recommending to him. He needed to get back on his feet. He can't protect his son from a hospital bed.

CHAPTER THIRTEEN

Callie placed Camico in his crib and rubbed his back until he stopped fussing and fell asleep. When she turned around, she was startled to see Calvin standing in the doorway of Camico's room.

"I'm sorry, I didn't mean to startle you. I wanted to be sure you're okay. Should you be lifting him? He's a pretty big boy and you look exhausted," Calvin said.

Callie rubbed her extended belly. She was days from delivering her baby and yet her priority was still to look after Camico even though they had two full-time nurses on staff to help out.

"I'm fine. This baby has been really active today and I think Camico is still excited being able to see you every day now. You've been here almost a month and the minute he wakes up and sees you, he is full throttle all day. We missed giving him a birthday party because you were still in Texas, but now that you're home, we need to have something for him," she said.

"We? You'll be dealing with your own baby in a day or two. I can hire someone to pull a party together for a one year old. It would only be us anyway, so I don't think it will take much," Calvin said.

"True. Either way, I want to be a part of it. This little guy has brought me so much joy and he's helped me prepare for this baby since I've been taking care of him for the past four months."

"Thanks for being here. I know it's a lot on you in your condition. How are you, by the way?" he asked.

"I'm fine. Cade wasn't happy I left the house to come here today to check on you and Camico, but I told him I was fine and I had a driver – no driving for me until well after the baby is born. Did Cade tell you it's a girl?" she said, beaming.

"He did and I'm happy for you. Without seeing it with my own eyes, I never pictured Cade married with a child on the way."

"I know. Believe me, I know exactly what your brother was like before I met him and I'm surprised myself that we fell in love, but we did and I have never been happier," she admitted.

"I've never seen my brother this happy. You are a wonder maker. You make him happier than I have ever seen him and happier than I think he thought he could ever be himself."

"We are perfect together. Don't forget the physical therapist will be here in an hour and your grandmother should be on her way back from the store. She wanted to be here before I left in case Camico woke up during your session. Are you sure you don't need me to stay?"

"I'm sure. This new therapist that Trey recommended is finally coming on board. She was completely booked up until this week. I've been working with someone else she recommended and now that we're getting to the intense part of the therapy, she's coming on board. I still find it hard that my brother is so domesticated. I mean, he was once labeled Hollywood's heartthrob and now he's married, about to be a father and made his home base in Texas and not in LaLa land! I'm happy he's happy," Cade said.

"I thought at one time we'd be making our home in Los Angeles. I still love going there, but I love being out of the limelight here in Texas. The few times paparazzi tried to accost me here, they had to deal with my father and his men and they wanted none of that. Cade granted the media access to him whenever he was anywhere, but here in Texas and because of that, they leave us alone."

"Even the groupies?" Calvin asked, laughing.

"That's another story. Women are just wretched. Thankfully, my husband loves me, is dedicated to me and happily gave up his playboy ways. There's nothing we can do about the groupies, but pregnant or not, I will shut them all down!" Callie declared.

"Sis, I believe you will."

"I see you're getting around good with those crutches," Callie said.

Calvin spent the first two weeks at home moving about in a wheelchair and had recently begun using two crutches. He was hoping to get down to one crutch soon. Due to his great physical condition, he was healing quickly.

"I am and having an elevator in my house makes it easier. Now that Camico is asleep, I'm going to go downstairs to wait for the physical therapist."

"Be easy on her. I hear you've been pretty rough on the others who've been working with you."

"Yes. There was a guy here the other day who assessed the equipment to be sure everything we would need was delivered and set up correctly based on her recommendation of what she thought we would need or the sessions. I promise to chill out and not unleash my frustration on anyone else. Trust me, my grandmother has already warned me," he laughed.

"You go ahead. I'm waiting for my sister to come pick me up. I'm gonna sit in this rocking chair until she gets here. After she dropped me off here at your house this morning, she went to check out some new samples for my upcoming evening wear line. I think your grandmother is downstairs making lunch."

"Good. I am starving. Thanks for helping me with Camico, but I want you to take it easy. He's a handful."

"I will."

Calvin made his way to the elevator that he'd had installed after his friend, Trey Maxwell, connected him with a company that specialized in custom home security and doomsday preparation. Though he wasn't preparing for the end of the world, he did want to make sure that his son was protected at all times. As part of the installation, he had an elevator put in, especially since he knew he would have problems using the stairs with his crutches.

Besides the elevator, he also had a panic room installed that contained entry doors hidden behind walls. The panic room had monitors installed that watched over every room in his four-bedroom, six-bathroom home.

The most important feature besides the high-tech security system was the access to the panic room. Depending on where he was in the house, he could access the secure space from hidden panels in his room and Camico's room on the top floor as well as the kitchen and family room on the main level. He needed to do more work outdoors, but most important was the security inside.

He was able to breathe a sigh of relief knowing that it was possible Valencio still had no idea of who he was. For that, he could ease up on his worry about Camico's safety. Still, anything was possible," he thought as he exited the elevator on the first floor. He wasn't paying attention when he walked toward the family room.

"Mister Lymon?" a voice said, startling him.

Calvin turned to greet the therapist, but the words hello got caught in his throat. He was expecting a more masculine woman after hearing she'd had four years of military experience along with her work as a physical therapist. Someone must have made a mistake because the woman standing in front of him could pass for any model someone would find on a runway.

She was shorter than he expected and appeared to be around five-foot six or seven, which was short compared to his six-foot-three stature. Her hair was pulled up into a tight ponytail, but if his assessment was correct and she was working with natural hair, he imagined it would fall down and flow about her shoulders. She was a dynamo and though she was dressed casually in a sweat suit for their session, he could imagine her in a tight slinky dress, flaunting the curves her suit failed to hide.

"Calvin!"

He jumped, startled, hearing the sound of his grandmother's shouting at him.

"Huh?" he said.

"Didn't you hear this young lady greet you? You're standing there staring at her like some crazed lunatic. Get it together," she laughed. "I'm going upstairs to check on Callie the baby. He should be up soon from his nap and will be hungry. I'll leave you to your session," she said walking away.

Snapping out of a daze, he walked over to his visitor on his crutches.

"I'm sorry about that. I don't know where my mind was. You're miss Cortez?" he asked.

"Yes, and please call me Ava."

"Well, only if you'll call me Cal or Calvin."

"Okay, I can do that. I'm here for your first session today. I was told you had an entire room you converted to a space that rivals any hospital rehab center. I'd like to see it and before we start, I have some questions I'd like to ask you. There's also some paperwork we need to go over before we start. I know you've been working with one of my partners. He tends to start things off and then when things get really intense, that's when I take over. Did the additional equipment arrive?" Ava asked watching Calvin as he moved, checking to see how his body moved.

"Yes, everything showed up and was set up earlier."

"Good. How does your leg feel and have you been doing any exercises the week you've been home and finally out of the wheelchair?" she asked.

"I've stuck to everything in the doctor's orders and the leg is feeling pretty good," he said.

"I hear you're a remarkable case considering how badly your leg was damaged from the gunshots," she said.

"That's what I hear. I'm not a man to be held

down for long and I plan to be back with my team one day – I just don't know when yet."

"I'm sorry that it looks like it will be months before you're even evaluated for light duty. It'll be a while before you return to your team and the active duty of a Navy SEAL."

"Well, that's not the real reason I don't know when I'll return. I have a year-old son and I can't imagine leaving him alone and going back to the work I was doing that kept me away from family for months at a time."

"I can understand that," she said. "Let's see this room and then we can talk a little about the plan for you after I see the progress you've made so far. That will tell me if I need to restructure your plan or not."

"Follow me," Calvin said and walked on his crutches ahead of her toward the room on the first floor that he and Cade had turned into a mini gym.

Ava could barely contain herself. She'd worked with military men before, but there was something special about Calvin that she felt an instant attraction to. That was something she'd never done before with a client, but Calvin was a special case. He was more than just handsome even on crutches. She watched him as he moved and couldn't help noticing the magnificent shape he was in. Being in the military once herself, she knew how buff military men could be, but Calvin was a cut above any she'd ever seen. He exceeded what would be considered handsome.

In the gray sweatpants and t-shirt, she could see all of his toned muscles from head to feet. His chest bulged in the form fitting tee and she couldn't miss the tight, taut shape of his physique from behind. She could tell from a quick glance that he took great care in how he looked, even while relaxed at home and walking around on crutches.

Looking at him, she felt a tingling sensation and knew that she was already crossing the line by seeing him as more than a client. For the first time in a long time, she was looking at a man and wondering what he looked like naked. Shaking off the thought, Ava tried to focus on the task at hand and that was assessing how far Calvin Lymon had progressed in therapy and how much more work she had to do. Focusing on his gorgeous attributes had to be put on the back burner.

Chapter Fourteen

Ava couldn't contain the smile on her face even if she wanted to when Calvin opened the door to let her in without the use of his cane.

"Surprise!"

"Surprise is right. You're walking without your cane. That's the greatest surprise ever!" she exclaimed.

For the past two months, they had worked to get him off of his crutches and after two weeks, he'd been down to one and from the looks of it, he not only no longer needed either crutch, he didn't even need the cane he'd began using a week ago.

Ava walked around him into the house for their session and turned to get an even better look at him.

"You look amazing," she said before she knew the impact of her words. She meant to tell him he looked amazingly sturdy standing and moving around on his own without his cane, but she stopped at the word amazing because deep down, that's exactly how she felt.

The past two months of working with Calvin had been the best of her life. She'd gained more than just a client, but they had actually become pretty good friends.

He'd listened to her woes about how busy her schedule was and the pains of running a thriving business and all the drama that entailed. He even gave her great advice on expanding her business and even connected her with some of Cade's business partners who gave her a helping hand with advice about some changes she needed to make that could increase her staff and her revenue.

What she also enjoyed was time spent with his son, Camico. She had grown to love seeing him when she came for Calvin's sessions. Despite what occurred in his life that hopefully he'll never remember, he was the happiest little boy and he loved his father very much. He was learning to talk and she was glad she was at the house the day he learned to say 'dada'. Calvin still talks about it as if he'd won the Nobel Peace Prize. To see them together had her wishing that one day, she'd have a little boy just like Camico and a loving, caring and gorgeous man like Calvin.

Despite the business aspect of their connection, there was something growing between them and as hard as they both tried to fight it, she could see they were too close to crossing a line. Everything in her was telling her to back off and remember why she was in his house almost daily, but temptation was a beast she was having a hard time taming. The beast in her wanted Calvin Lymon in the worst way and each time they were together, she used all of her strength to resist flirting with him even though he'd turned up his charm, appeal and zest for flirting with her.

Calvin was damn near irresistible especially when he smiled at her with those perfectly aligned pearly whites. His smile could get anything from anyone and she was no exception. She found herself compromising in ways she knew she shouldn't.

During a few of their sessions, she stayed around and had either lunch or an early dinner with him and his son. After betting her that he could do more than fifty leg presses, he'd won and his prize was on her next visit, she had to bring a bathing suit to join him in the hot tub. He was supposed to be using it to soothe his aching bones and joints after their sessions, but that day, they relaxed and talked about fun things like going through lists of their favorite things. They discovered they had a lot of them in common, something else that had her even more drawn to him.

"You look amazing, too," Calvin said.

Ava had been thinking so hard about what had been transpiring between them over the weeks, she saw his lips moving, but didn't hear the words.

"What?" she asked.

"I said, you look amazing, too. I mean the words,

but I didn't know what else to do since for a few minutes, you seemed to check out. What were you thinking about so hard?" he asked.

Ava turned and walked further into the house.

"Truth?" she said with her back to him.

"Truth always," Calvin replied following her into the home gym.

Dropping her bag on the floor, Ava turned to face him.

"I was thinking about our time over the past few months and how much I've enjoyed helping you get your strength back. Seeing you walk around without your cane reminded me that our time will be up in a few more weeks. I'm going to miss seeing you and Camico."

"Miss us? Where are you going?" he asked.

"You won't need a therapist forever. Look at you. You're doing good and no cane today. That's a major hurdle. Have you been speed walking like I recommended?" she asked.

"I've been doing better than that. I actually did a little jogging this morning and it felt great. I have a little pain, but that's expected. I took Camico out to let him walk around and keeping up with him, I was forced to job. That kid of mine has Lymon energy. I am a little sore from that, but otherwise, I'm feeling pretty good."

"We'll work that pain out today, so don't worry," she said.

"I never worry when I'm in your care. I know our

sessions will end soon, but I hope that doesn't mean the end of Camico and I seeing you. Maybe I can talk you into having dinner with me soon."

Calvin was taking a leap and knew it would mean crossing a line, but he didn't care. There was no way, therapist or not, was he going to let Ava walk out of his life.

He appreciated all she'd done to get him back up on his feet and finally walking without the use of crutches or a cane. Now that he was close to recovery where he would no longer need as much time with a therapist, he was hoping to take their friendship to the next level.

Being real with himself, he had begun seeing Ava as more than his therapist immediately after they'd met. As soon as she walked into his house that first day, he had been in awe of her ever since. She was not only at the top of her game as a therapist, but over the past few months, he'd come to know more about her and loved everything he was discovering.

He loved that they laughed all the time about silly things and during his sessions, though their focus was on his care, he was able to talk to her about everything, including what happened to him that landed him in the need of care. The way she attentively listened and showed how much she was really concerned about him drew him to her. She was beautiful, powerful and all woman. She was sexy whether she wore a sweat suit, her usual attire or if she had on a business suit when she stopped by to check on him while on her way to one meeting or another.

After the first few days, she showed up for his session with her long hair flowing down around her shoulders and he couldn't stop looking at her. A few times he had actually stumbled because he was more focused on her beauty than on his steps.

She had shared with him the drama around what happened to her and her siblings and how they survived with the help of Trey and Dustin, who were also friends of his. Sometimes after his sessions, he was able to convince her to hang around and enjoy a meal with him. Days when Camico was home, he loved playing hide and seek with Ava though he didn't yet understand the idea of hiding meant he shouldn't be seen. To him, as long as he covered his face, he didn't think anyone could see him. Ava found that hilarious and he loved her interaction with him.

For a few days, Camico was staying at Cade's house when his grandparents came to town to help him and Callie with the new baby who made her arrival on time two months ago. Little miss Colby Weston was getting everyone's attention and from what he was told, Camico was fascinated with his little cousin.

"So, how is Callie doing?" Ava asked as they entered the gym and she set equipment up.

"She's doing good. She hasn't come out of the house yet, but she sends me pictures of the baby every day. My grandparents took Camico with them and are staying at Cade's for a few days. Cade is filming a movie here in Texas so most days, he's on set now and they wanted to be here to help. She thought she was going to have to go through withdrawal and not see Camico for a while after she had the baby, but she's good since he's been there the past week. I hear he missed her as much as she missed him."

"Who's here helping you?" she asked.

"I don't need any help. I'm getting around fine. I have someone who comes in to cook and clean and my grandparents come by to check on me and then there is you," he said softly.

"Me?"

"You're more than my therapist. I consider you a friend," he said.

Ava tried to avoid eye contact because over the past two months, she had become totally enthralled by Calvin and didn't know how to handle it.

"We are friends."

Calvin moved closer to her.

"Could you see us as more than friends?" he asked. He didn't want to make her feel uncomfortable, but their time together and getting to know each other, he wanted her and deep down, he had a feeling it was mutual. The only thing that stood in their way was her desire to remain professional with him. He wanted that notion out the window.

It had been a long time since he'd thought about anything other than getting better, but now that he was well on his way to mending, his mind turned to how his body reacted every time they were around each other. He couldn't help that he found everything about her to be sexy. He would often catch himself looking at her sexy curves and when she bent over, his eyes went straight to her round, yet firm backside and all he could do was imagine what she would look like naked and thrashing around under him.

Even now, thoughts of her was causing his body to harden. That part of him that he didn't want to show and embarrass himself was also hardening and he willed it to go back to being pliant. Ava seemed to always have that impact on him and he was tired of dancing around his want for her.

He noticed she didn't answer his last question and assumed he'd caught her off guard. He hoped and prayed that he wasn't making her uncomfortable.

"Are you ready to begin?" she asked.

"Ava? Did you hear my question or are you ignoring me?" Calvin asked, sitting down on the work bench. He tried to remain casual, but the way his nights were set up, he could no longer continue as if he wasn't interested in her.

When their sessions were over and he found himself in bed, unable to sleep, she was often on his mind. He was well aware that he was her patient and he shouldn't venture into territory that could compromise her professional standing with him, but he was far beyond wanting to remain professional. Ava was much more than that and inside, he could see her struggle with feelings he assumed she was developing for him. Why should they fight it?

While securing his workout gloves that enabled him to grip equipment better, he waited for her to respond, though she wouldn't look at him.

"You know I can't answer that," she finally said.

"Why not? Am I wrong for thinking that there is a vibe happening between us? If I'm making you uncomfortable, tell me and I'll stop."

"That's not it at all."

"Then what is it? The fact that you're my therapist and I'm your client? I don't care about that," he said.

"I do."

"What if you happen to find that a client is the man you desire? Do you walk away from that because of an invisible ethics line? We're adults, Ava."

When she turned toward him, finally looking in his eyes, he found himself lost in the dark pools that stared back at him.

"Yes, I find you attractive, but I can't go there, whether I wanted to or not."

"Does that mean I'm not the only one with the inward struggle? Come on, don't leave me out here on my own. There is something happening between us that's not just client and therapist or just friends – there is something much more than that and I know you sense it. I think about you all the time and I don't want to stop."

"Don't Calvin," Ava said.

"Okay, I'll stop because I can see this isn't a good subject. I want you to know that if there is a chance that you'd go out with me, I hope you'll tell me and not run from anything we might feel," he said.

Ava exhaled deeply and tried her best to focus on the task at hand. She wasn't ready to confront the fact that whenever she left his house, he was all she could think about. At night, she had sexy thoughts and dreams about him that had her waking up in the morning all sweaty, pretty much satisfied from the hot moments in her dream with him starring in every one of them.

As Ava reached for the leg weights to place around his legs, Calvin tried to again make eye contact. Without making the air between them more intense, he let the subject drop and focused on his treatment.

An hour later and totally exhausted, Calvin walked Ava to the door after she declined his invitation to join him for lunch. He had a feeling it was because throughout their session, this was the first time they didn't engage in idle chatter.

"Thanks for today's session. Same time in two days?" he asked. "Camico will be here and he'll be happy to see you," he added.

"I can't wait to see him. I've missed him these last few sessions."

Once they reached the door, Calvin placed his hand on the door handle without opening the door. Ava's back was to him as he waited for her to turn around and talk to him directly.

"Look at me," he said in a deep, husky voice. He couldn't let her leave with an uneasy air between them.

Slowly Ava turned and the moment their eyes locked, all thought of avoiding the inevitable was lost. Neither of them spoke as they kept eyes on each other. Calvin could feel his breaths deepen as the only thought on his mind was about how delicious he knew her lips would taste and feel against his.

Not taking his eyes away, he leaned closer, slowly giving her a chance to move away knowing what was coming.

"So beautiful," he said and before she had a chance to respond and before his next breath, he kissed her. It wasn't a sweet, soft kiss like he planned, but it was hot and titillating, causing them both to moan. He reached out and pulled her snug into his arms as he deepened the kiss that they were now equally engaged in.

He felt dizzy with need the moment their mouths touched. He felt like he was about to erupt the moment their tongues touched and then mated.

The zealousness by which they were devouring each other signed, sealed and delivered confirmation to him that he was falling for Ava. The moment he felt another moan surfacing, Ava pulled away. He watched her touch her lips where his had just been and the moment turned awkward.

"We shouldn't have done that," she said and turned to leave as she grabbed the door handle and opened it.

"I'm sorry," he said.

Ava didn't say anything as she walked out. Before getting in her car in the circle in front of the house, she turned back to him.

"I'll see you and Camico on Thursday," she said.

With that, Ava was gone and Calvin knew he'd crossed a dangerous line. He wanted her, but he never wanted her to regret kissing him and regret was exactly what he saw when the kiss ended. He didn't mean to make her uncomfortable, but his desire for her took over all common sense.

Following a cold shower, he knew was in store for him, he needed to think through what he would say to her next.

~~

Valencio was excited that he had finally been able to reach his contact in the United States. He still didn't know the identity of the soldier who admitted that he was Camico's father and that he had him, but information that he was a soldier would make it easier to find him.

His contact, someone he had paid millions to over the past few years was working to get him into the country where he would spend day and night looking for his grandson who he believed was there. His father was an American soldier and the congressman who was on his payroll was working hard to find out the names of the SEAL team members, though it wasn't information that was shared even in the highest levels of government to protect their identities.

After months of getting his affairs back in order at a new secret location underground, Valencio was now ready to seek his revenge and get his grandson back. Camico was all he had left in the world and no one was going to keep him from getting him back.

Reaching for his phone, he dialed the congressman's number to find out how much longer he would have to wait to get into the United States undetected. It was time to reclaim what was his.

"I'm coming for you, Camico. Poppy hasn't forgotten about you," he said and sneered.

CHAPTER FIFTEEN

Calvin smiled uneasily as Ava walked toward him as he stood in his doorway after she parked her car. He was surprised, yet happy to see her. He assumed after the move he made a few days ago after their session, that she would probably send someone else for his session. He had called her twice, once that night and again the day before and she didn't answer or call him back. He decided to wait to see what would happen for his session scheduled for Thursday.

He was getting around good and the day before, he had actually run a mile with no pain. On one level, he was disappointed considering in the past, he could easily run ten miles and feel exhilarated afterwards. He didn't want to press his luck, though he was feeling a lot better and the leg gave him little pain.

Scanning Ava's face for any sign that her being here would be uncomfortable, he saw none and perked up when she gave him a bright smile.

"You're looking strong standing on those legs," Ava said coming to stand right in front of him.

"I'm actually feeling really good. I took your advice and did only a mile run yesterday. I could have done more, but you're right, I shouldn't push it, so I didn't. It's good to see you."

Calvin wanted to say more, but was hesitant. He was sure the same encounter they'd had a few days ago was fresh on her mind as it was on his. No matter how hard he tried to forget about the kiss they shared, he couldn't. He wasn't sure he wanted to. The kiss had crossed the line, one he should never have crossed, but the need to taste her was greater than common sense. The months of working together had shown a light on how much he wanted her.

At first, he thought it was pure lust, but the moment his lips touched hers, he knew he was developing deeper feelings for her than just something casual. Something in him said that Ava had been feeling the growing connection, but unlike him, she'd done a good job fighting it.

"It's good to be seen. I saw Callie's car leaving. I didn't realize she was coming out yet after having the baby. Is Camico okay? I know how she is about him."

"Camico is fine. He was supposed to come home today, but Callie was going to her sister's house for a while for her first outing with Colby and she wanted to take Camico with her. She stopped by for him to see me. He'll be home tomorrow. I wanted to get a hug and a kiss from him. I was really missing my little man the few days he's been gone."

"I was hoping to see him today," Ava said as she walked up to him.

"You look beautiful today," Calvin said and waited to see if the moment would be odd.

"Thank you."

"I wasn't sure you would show up today," he admitted.

"Why wouldn't I show up?" she asked.

"The kiss? I was sure you wouldn't want to see me again. You left here with a look of terror on your face. I called you a few times and you didn't answer or call me back. I felt the need to apologize for making you feel uncomfortable."

"I wasn't uncomfortable. I was more surprised than anything and I needed to digest what happened which is why I didn't call you back. I knew I'd see you today."

"Here I was, worried all day that you would send someone else for our last few sessions and you'd be gone. I didn't want that. Are you going to ask me to hide the fact that I'm falling for you?" he asked, being honest. If they were only going to have a few more sessions together, he wanted to put all of the cards on the table.

"Are we going to stand out here in this heat and talk or are we still on for your session today?" Ava asked, standing before him looking nervous though she didn't take her eyes off of his. She understood how he was feeling because she was feeling the same way. She'd come to the conclusion in the few days since their last session.

She had thought about sending another staff member for Calvin's session today, but decided against it. Her priority was making sure he was healing and now was not the time to hand him off to someone else. She could deal with her attraction to him. What she was struggling with was his attraction to her. She could keep her feelings under wrap if she needed to, but knowing that he was open and honest about his, brought hers to the surface and that scared her. She wanted him as much as he wanted her and that scared her not only on the level as his therapist, but because it had been a few years since she'd had any feelings for a man, yet with Calvin, she had fallen hard and didn't know how to handle it in the professional setting.

"Of course. Come on in. I wasn't sure we would have a session today or at least that you wouldn't be doing the session today, but I'm glad we are."

Ava walked past him into the house and walked toward his gym.

"Why wouldn't we have a session? You only have three more and then I should be able to clear you."

"I don't know. I really thought after what happened the other day that you'd run for the hills and send someone else to finish my sessions out. I meant what I said when I told you I was sorry. I didn't mean to cross any lines."

Ava turned to him when she was halfway into the room and he stood at the entrance.

"Calvin, I won't let anything like a kiss keep me from doing my job, though I've never been kissed by a client in that way before."

Calvin smiled.

"There have been other kisses before?" he asked, jokingly. He smiled when she smiled at him.

"Not like that. Just friendly hugs and kisses on the cheek, but no lip action. You were my first for that."

"So, your first for lip action or your first for lip action from a client?" he asked and laughed before she could answer. He hoped she was finding as much humor in their chat as he was. He wanted to lighten the mood and not dwell on his mistake.

"Very funny. You know what I mean. Now, no more talk about that day. It's in the past and we've been working so closely together that something like that can happen. I won't let it keep me from doing my job."

Calvin walked in closer to her.

"Does it matter to you that I find you extremely attractive, beyond beautiful and though I apologized for making you uncomfortable that day, I'm not sorry that I kissed you? I've wanted to do that for several weeks and I couldn't stand to wait anymore. I would never take advantage of you or the situation and for a few seconds, I felt like it was something you wanted as well with the way you were kissing me back."

"Are we going to spend your session talking about this?"

"Am I making you uncomfortable? If so, we can drop it," Calvin said. He didn't really want to drop the subject because as much as she may want to move beyond what happened, it was going to always be there until they no longer saw each other after his sessions, something else he was hoping to remedy.

Ava didn't respond at first. Calvin watched for any sign that the moment was awkward and wasn't sure what to expect when she walked back up to him. When she exhaled loudly, he thought that she was about to hit him with one of those, 'it's me, not you' kind of responses. He waited through what was clearly deep thinking occurring on her part.

"I'm not uncomfortable and I would be lying if I said I didn't enjoy the kiss. I did and I'll even admit I had thought about what it would be like to kiss you. I pushed that thought into the back of my mind because I am here to do a job, not jump my client. You are a very handsome man and any woman would be lying if she said she didn't find you attractive, almost irresistible, but again, I have a job to do and when I'm on the clock, I can't cross the line with you. I have never done that and I never will again. Now, can we get to this session and drop the chat about the kiss. It was a kiss, not my first and not yours and now it's over," she said confidently.

Ava smiled and turned away as she walked over to the mat and dropped her backpack down.

"Wait? I'm irresistible? I like that."

Ava shook her head and he laughed.

"You are certifiable, Calvin."

"That I am, but I'm also very much attracted to you and I don't know how or that I would want to turn that off. Now, you said no kissing while on the clock. What about when you're not on the clock? Can I ask you out to maybe dinner or a movie then?" he asked.

"Calvin Lymon, get over here and get your stretches started. We have a lot of work to do today."

Glad that any amount of awkwardness had passed, Calvin walked over to the mat and started the session.

"I'm just saying, if I find you attractive and you find me irresistible, I think we should see where this goes," he said as he started stretching while Ava watched him for any signs of pain or struggle.

"Any leg pains?" she asked.

"No, none."

Calvin continued to stretch, moving his leg in a variety of ways to test the boundaries.

After several bullets passed through it and two lodging in it that were eventually removed, he was lucky he hadn't loss the leg. He was more than grateful for the team of doctors who were responsible for his care. Most of all, he was thankful for Ava, who helped bring him back to life. He had spent so much time mourning Sofia, worrying about her father who was still on the loose and worried about his career as a SEAL that he couldn't focus on anything else.

Camico's love and need for him was his number one priority, but he didn't think he would find himself attracted to his therapist and it was more than just a physical attraction. Over the past few months, Ava had become an important part of his life. As he continued with his routine, he thought of the many things they'd shared with each other and how it had drawn them to each other.

"You're doing good. I think you'll be ready to be cleared after our last two sessions and then you can finally get rid of me and the way I order you around. That won't mean you'll be able to return to duty, but you can exercise more and get back to a more regular routine."

"I like having you order me around. Only two sessions left, huh?" he asked.

Ava tried to look away from Calvin's handsome face, but his light brown eyes drew her in like a moth to a flame. To say that Calvin was handsome was actually an understatement. She knew that his brother, Cade, at one time had been labeled a heartthrob, the world's sexiest man, but to her, Calvin beat him out for that title, hands down.

She loved his chocolate brown skin and the way he flexed his muscles, if he were her man, she'd love to see him walk around all day without a shirt on.

From the first day she saw pictures him all battered and bruised from his injuries, she felt a ping of excitement flow through her body that she'd never experienced before. Even in that condition, he was still the finest man she'd ever seen.

Due to her situation before moving to Texas, she kept her dating life to a minimum in order to protect her life and the lives of her sister and brother. She didn't want anyone diving too far into who she was and so other than good friends like Mackenzie and other women at the hospital where she worked, she kept her interactions to a small group of people. Now that she was once again free to live her life openly, she wanted nothing more than to be involved with a hot, sexy man like Calvin, but what she didn't expect was to have feelings for a client, something she had always been particular about. Calvin was different and though she tried with everything in her to tamper down her desire for him, she could feel herself losing the battle the more time they spent around each other.

As she watched Calvin go through the routine to test the strength of his legs, she couldn't help but think back to the kiss they shared. She couldn't say she had been caught off guard because he gave her a few seconds to say no or to back up as he moved closer and closer to her lips. Instead of doing either, she let her eyes drift down from his eyes to his lips as her heart sped up knowing she was about to be kissed by the man who had been starring in her dreams for the past few weeks and in those dreams, they did more than kiss. When she woke in the morning, her body was hot like fire for him. Her desire for him was getting the best of her.

Who does that? She thought. Who lusts after their client knowing it's a dangerous line to cross and she prided herself on being ethically sound. Never in her career has she ever crossed a line with someone, but with Calvin she had been tempted and the kiss didn't help any. That night after returning home, she had been up half the night thinking about him, touching herself and imagining it was his hands all over her body. She'd had to kick the blankets off of her when the heat that radiated from her body had he bed feeling like she was laying on a bed of hot coals.

"Focus, Calvin," she said when she noticed him watching her and no longer working on his form. She should know since her mind and eyes were all over his form and if she weren't careful, she would find herself being the one initiating a kiss with him this time.

"You want me," Calvin said and Ava doubled over laughing so hard.

"Again, you are certifiable," she said smiling.

"At least you didn't say I was wrong," he said. "When our sessions are officially done, does that mean you're gone forever? You'll miss Camico," he said, trying to get her to admit she didn't want to stop seeing him even though their professional association will be over.

She looked at him and smiled.

"Yes, I will miss Camico and I'll also miss Camico's father."

Calvin perked up.

"So, come on and put us both out of our misery and go out with me on a personal level."

Ava paused and looked up to the ceiling as she thought.

"Let me think about it. Right now, we need to focus."

"Focusing," he said, hopeful that he was making progress with her.

CHAPTER SIXTEEN

Valencio ventured from his hiding place inside the large estate in the Colorado mountains after a month of seclusion after his arrival in the United States. He was glad to finally be on American soil where he knew his grandson was living, but he didn't have a clue where.

As he walked out on the snow-covered hills, he turned around when he reached the railing and looked up at the large, sprawling estate that had been his home for the past few weeks. He looked through the large glass paned window at his men who gathered around a table, chowing down on various Italian dishes cooked by the staff of the United States military commander who was responsible for smuggling him into the country. He smiled at the thought that it was good to have men on his payroll in high positions in the U.S. government who had no problem compromising their morals for the all-mighty dollar. Nothing was going to keep him from finding the man who had gotten his daughter pregnant and stolen his grandson away. Now was his time to seek revenge for not only his daughter's death, but the death of his only son. He would still have them both if this American soldier hadn't gotten mixed up with his daughter. She wouldn't have been caught in the middle of the military's mission gone wrong.

After months of living underground in South America knowing he was a hunted man, he lived in the darkest, dirtiest places of the country until he felt it was safe to surface again. Thankful to those who would always remain loyal to him, he was nursed back to health and lived for the day he could seek his revenge and kill the man who brought mayhem into his life.

In the midst of his men enjoying their meal, he gave a head nod to the Admiral who returned the greeting. Though the Admiral thought he was in charge, he smirked knowing the Admiral was as far from being correct as one could get. No one controlled Valencio Ramirez and no one ever would.

Like everyone else in his circle, he served a purpose and when he is no longer needed, he'll be disposed of or perhaps turned over to his own country as a traitor. He had enough video and audio recorded conversations that could get the Admiral a death sentence. For now, he was the only link to finding his grandson and so he was essential.

He still held the Admiral responsible for not

giving him a warning that his compound was going to be raided. The reason for paying him huge sums of money under the table was so that he could be forewarned of any impending danger. That raid caught him off guard and it's possible the Admiral didn't know because his country was already suspicious of him. Why else would he not have been told about the mission? Valencio didn't like the idea that the Admiral may have been compromised, but for now, he was able to get smuggled into the U.S. without raising any red flags. That was the first step in finding his grandson.

The little bit of information he was finally able to gather was from a friend of Sofia's named Pierre, who had finally been tortured within inches of his life. All he knew was that Sofia had been involved with an American and he was a soldier. That he had discovered during the raid when the American soldier told him he was Camico's father right before he hit him with a hail of gunfire. In the exchange, he had also been shot, but was able to escape through underground tunnels that he'd spent millions building and concealing from any equipment that could discover them.

Pierre didn't know the soldier's real identity, but did give up that the soldier's name was no Leo as had been told to him by Sofia. No doubt, she did so to keep him off track. With the help of the Admiral, he would soon have a name to go with the covered face and looked forward to putting a bullet between them.

He tried without success to find Antonia who he believed had been lying to him when he asked her about the man Sofia had been seeing. Pierre told him that Antonia had helped Sofia sneak off to spend time with this American. By the time he was given that information, Antonia had disappeared. Word must have gotten back to her that he was looking for her. She was the missing link to him finding the identity of the soldier and now she was gone in the wind. He still had people looking for her, but now that he was on American soil, his focus was on finding the soldier.

He had a feeling the Admiral was stalling and bilking him for more and more money, but not producing any leads. The soldier should be easy to find considering he had to be severely wounded in the gunfire exchange. It shouldn't be hard to find a soldier who had been on a secret mission in South America with several gunshots. He was told all military bases and hospitals had been checked and he was unable to find any information. It appears he wasn't the only person who knew people in high places. This soldier had major connections if he was able to go off the grid with no trace.

The same is said for the location of his grandson. How was the soldier who was injured able to get Camico out of South America without a trace? According to his sources, though they were able to find a passport had been obtained by Sofia for

Camico, there was no record of it being used. Could Camico still be in South America? He didn't want to dwell too hard on it because he was able to get out of the country without the need for his passport, so it was possible. All he wanted now was to kill this American and to get his grandson back.

Walking back into the house he sat back down at the table as all eyes turned to him.

"So, Admiral, what's the latest?" he asked. "I've been here long enough for you to get me the information I need on this soldier. It's been months and other than you getting me into your country, nothing else has surfaced."

Valencio waited patiently as the Admiral took another bite of his baked lasagna, wiped his mouth, sipped some wine and then turned to him.

"Well, there has been a lot of security around that mission and the names of the soldiers involved are under lock and key. I'm getting closer based on any SEAL who didn't return to duty since you said he was injured."

Valencio was losing patience. He thought he could count on the Admiral, but so far, no luck. He was beginning to wonder if the Admiral was actually more loyal to his own country than he thought and was possibly dangling him on a string. In frustration, he banged on the table and stood, startling everyone.

"This man has my grandson and I want him found. I can't stay under the radar too long in this country. If I'm discovered, it could mean trouble for you, too. Now, find my grandson and find this soldier who knocked up my daughter and was a part of this raid on my house. I want him dead. Is that clear?" Valencio shouted.

He watched as the Admiral wiped his mouth again and stood.

"I'm getting on it. I have some leads that I'm expecting tonight. The few clues that boy, Pierre, gave you helped a lot. It's only been a few weeks since he gave that up and I'm working hard on this for you. You have to be patient. You're safe as long as you stay here. This place is secluded and there is only one way up this part of the mountain and there are men covering that road. No one knows you're here and if I was able to use my connections to get you here from South America, I can keep you safe here. I'm going to go see about this lead and I'll be in touch. In the meantime, don't forget about the next payment. I assume I should still be expecting that today?" Admiral Munson asked.

Valencio saw fire when he looked at him. How dare this minion ask him about money when his grandson's well-being was at stake. He spoke through clinched teeth.

"You'll have your money like I promised. You find my grandson, you money hungry leech. You Americans are so greedy, you would sell your children for a dollar," he said.

Valencio watched as the Admiral turned slowly

in his direction with a glaring look on his face.

"Are you going to talk to me about greed when it comes to children after what I hear you did to your own daughter? I hear you used her as a human shield? Is correct?"

In dire disgust, Valencio reached for his gun and pointed it at the Admiral's head.

"Don't you dare talk about my daughter – EVER!" he screamed. "I will put a bullet right between your beady little eyes," he added as a deep hatred for the Admiral seeped through him. His anger grew when Munson laughed at him.

"Do that and you'll never see your grandson. I'm the only connection to finding him right now, so I suggest you not forget that you may be in charge in South America, but in this country, you answer to me. Now, I'm going to do what you're paying me handsomely for and you worry about getting my money. You turned out to be more trouble than I anticipated when we made a deal several years ago. I agreed to help you get your drugs and weapons into this country and you agreed to pay me a lot of money for that. Keep doing that and I'll keep helping you. I would hate for word to get out that you're here and this place gets surrounded by more men than you saw enter your compound. Before you get a chance to say a word, you'd be dead. They don't want you taken alive, they want to see your dead body riddled with bullets and your life snuffed out. I am the only thing keeping you alive right now, so be careful when you pull a gun on your gift horse," the Admiral said.

Before Valencio could respond, he watched the Admiral leave the room and within seconds, he heard the front door slam. Gathering his thoughts and controlling his anger, he spoke pointedly.

"When this is over and I have my grandson, I want him dead. No one talks to Valencio Ramirez like that. Dead, is that clear?" he asked and locked eyes with all six men at the table.

"Crystal clear," they said in unison.

CHAPTER SEVENTEEN

"Callie, are you sure you don't want me to come and get him? Once he started walking, he hates sitting still and will scream if anyone tries to make him sit down," Calvin said.

"I know, he loves to not only walk, but he's trying to run fast and even though he keeps falling, he gets right back up and keeps on going. You have one ball of fire in Camico. He's fine here. Now that you're getting around more and back to driving, go do something for you and enjoy a little free time," Callie said.

Calvin had called her at the end of his latest session with Ava to see if she needed a break from Camico. With her hands full with her own baby now, he knew Camico had to be giving her a run for her money. His family had really stepped up to the plate to help him raise his son. Not a day went by that he didn't look at his son and see his mother. He still carried a lot of blame for what happened to Sofia, but thankfully, Camico hasn't missed a beat.

There is so much love around him that he knew he can't help but thrive. He was focused on giving him the life his mother always wanted him to have, one that was far away from what her life was like growing up with Valencio.

"Okay, if you're sure. Is Cade back yet?" he asked.

Cade had flown out to California to take care of some business, promising to only be gone for a few days.

"He's still in Los Angeles, but he'll be back next weekend for the first showing of the movie he shot here in Texas. We're showing it to close family and friends here at the house. Are you still coming?" she asked.

"I wouldn't miss an opportunity to see my brother in action. I'm already hearing this one will top all of the charts. My grandparents are coming back for the showing. Did Cade tell you they asked if there were any scenes that they should be aware of before they view the movie?" he asked.

He laughed out loud when Callie choked on the other end, trying to suppress a laugh.

"He did and told me they were referencing any sex scenes. He said he told them it's an action movie and little to no bare skin, especially for him. He's the star that looks amazing fully clothed and in expensive, tailored suits. He told them it's safe. What are you going to do with this free time to yourself?" she asked.

Calvin looked over at Ava as she gathered up her equipment and attempted to straighten up the room now that they were finished for the day. Their session was over and she was preparing to leave. He hoped he could talk her into staying around a while and joining him for an early dinner his cook had prepared earlier in the day and left for him to heat up later. After giving his staff the weekend off, he had been planning to relax and do some shopping for Camico who was already growing out of his clothes. Callie often had outfits delivered that she either had made or bought for Camico and he was already growing out of some of those.

What he wanted most was to spend some time with Ava when they weren't focused on his therapy sessions. He wanted personal one on one time with her. She still had not answered his question about going out on a date with him when he asked a week ago.

He eyed her as she moved about putting the mats back in place and moving the weights she could lift. She was a beautiful woman and he knew if he didn't try hard before his last session, he may not get another chance. Next week would be their last session together. He was running out of time. Maybe Callie could help him with his approach.

He'd always been the type of guy who was never ready to commit to one woman. He traveled all over the world and any woman he hooked up with knew nothing would come out of it. With Sofia, he was still all military, but he loved her. With Ava, he wanted much more. He wanted love and commitment and he was willing to do anything to get her to believe he was serious about her.

"I'm going to step out for a second. Don't leave yet, okay?" he said to Ava. When she turned toward him, his desire heightened. If he wasn't careful, he may have to admit he was falling in love with her.

"I'll be right here," she said.

Calvin left the room and walked into the kitchen for some privacy and turned his attention back to Callie on the phone.

"I'm not doing much, but relaxing, getting in some extra exercise to continue strengthening up my legs. I was planning on doing a little shopping for some things for Camico now that I'm back to driving. Listen, I've never had a sister and you're the closest to that I'll ever get. I need to ask you something," Calvin said, speaking softly so that Ava couldn't hear.

"What's wrong? Is everything okay?" she asked.

"Yes. It's more of a personal thing," he said.

"Is this about, Ava?" she asked.

Calvin held the phone out and looked at it, surprised that she knew what the topic was without him saying it.

"What is this sixth-sense that women have? It's spooky!" he said.

"It doesn't take all that for anyone to see you have a thing for her. Cade also mentioned it to me.

He asked if at any time when I've been by your house to visit or pickup up Camico, if I've seen anything fishy going on between you two."

"Damn! Is it that obvious?" he asked.

"It is and I understand why. I've had the chance to talk with her sometimes and I really like her. She's a nice woman and of course, she's beautiful, that goes without needing to be said. Tell me what's up," Callie said.

Calvin smiled. "I do like her – a lot. I think I may have crossed a line by kissing her a few days ago during one of my sessions. It bothered her and she ran out of here making me scared that I took a liberty with her that I should not have. Since then, I can't think of anything, but her. I want to see her outside of her being my therapist, but I don't know how to approach it without her feeling like she's doing something wrong because I'm her client. I only have one session left and I don't want her to walk out of my life. Is that crazy?" he asked.

"No, it's not crazy at all. If you really feel deeply about her, don't let her walk away. Do you know if she is interested in you?"

"Callie, she kissed me back with so much passion, I think that's what scared her. It wasn't that we kissed, but that she was giving into a feeling she had been holding back. I don't want her to hold it back from me if I'm not in this alone. I don't want to go about this the wrong way and push her away," he admitted.

"If she feels anything like what you're feeling, you won't push her away. Talk to her about what you're feeling. The only way you'll know if what you feel will lead to anything is to talk it out and let her know there is nothing that says she can't find a great man in a client. I may be one-sided in my opinion, but you are a great guy. You deserve to have each other if what you feel is real."

Calvin paused, then spoke.

"It's as real as real can get. Thanks, Callie and remember if Camico gets to be too much, I'm a phone call away. I don't know how you women do it. That son of mine tires me out chasing him around this house. He only calms down for you and Grams."

Callie laughed.

"That's because we women have that magical touch and he'll be fine. My sister and her husband are here visiting and the minute my father heard Camico was here, he and my mom are coming over to the house for dinner. Your son loves my father and that feeling is mutual. We are so happy to have him in our lives. I would have loved to meet Sofia, but she is smiling in heaven knowing you are taking good care of him and that he has a family that will love and spoil him. Now, I heard you talking to Ava, so get back to her and I'll see you on Sunday when I drop your son off."

Calvin could hear Camico laughing in the background.

"I can hear him laughing," he said.

"My sister is pushing him on the swing Cade had installed. When I told him Colby wasn't big enough to put in a swing yet, he told me it was for Camico. Your brother is just as bad as me when it comes to spoiling your son."

"I still can't believe I have a son. He is my heartbeat. Never in my wildest dreams did I ever imagine being a father right now. I wouldn't trade it for anything," he said.

"I can and he's looking like you more and more every day. Except for that head full of curly black hair and his lighter skin, he would be your twin."

"Yeah, that hair and skin color he gets from his mother. Everything else about him is all me. I'll see you Sunday and thanks for the ear, sis," he said.

"Love you, brother," Callie said and hung up.

Calvin sat his cell phone on the kitchen counter and went back into his gym to join Ava who had turned on the stereo system in the room and was singing along with a Whitney Houston song. He stood in the doorway and listened without disturbing her. When she turned and saw him staring, she stopped singing.

"Don't stop on my account," he said. "You have a beautiful voice. I didn't know you could sing," he added.

"There's a lot you don't know about me," she said.

"I'd love to remedy that if you give me the

chance to."

"Calvin, is this about that kiss again?" Ava asked.

He walked further into the room.

"No, this isn't about the kiss. This is about me and you on a level that has nothing to do with you as my therapist. Can we talk for a few minutes before you leave? Actually, I was hoping I could convince you to stay a while and have dinner with me if you didn't have plans when you left here."

When Ava didn't immediately respond, he was afraid she was coming up with a way to let him down.

"You're not going to let this go, huh?" she asked.

"Do you want me to let it go? Am I the only one feeling a connection beyond therapist and client here? If so, then I'll let it go if that's what you want, though it's not what I want. I want to see you outside of being my therapist. When you're off the clock, I want to take you out to dinner or anything else we could get into together. We've been client and therapist for four months now and I appreciate all that you've done. Now that I'm close to getting back to some semblance of normalcy, I want the next level. I want to spend some time with Ava Cortez the woman, not the therapist. Am I wrong for that?" he asked as he reached out and took one of her hands into both of his. He wanted to be close to her so that she could see how deeply he meant what he was saying. "Is what I'm saying one-sided?" he added.

Ava looked down to where their hands were joined and then looked back up at him. When she looked into his eyes, she saw sincerity. She looked into eyes that she fell asleep to every night in her mind. He had been what she thought about when she was alone.

She tossed between her desire for him and her duty to her profession and the idea of never crossing the line with a client. She's had other clients who developed a liking for her, but this was the first time she felt the same way. Did she really want to just walk away?

"It's not one-sided, but I'm scared. I've never developed feelings for a client before, ever and I don't know what to do about it now."

"You go with it. There's nothing wrong with what we're feeling for each other. I welcome it from you and I hope you feel the same way. What we feel has nothing to do with what you do – it's about who you are and that, my sweet, is a beautiful, desirable woman and I want to get to know more and more about you. I know you have reservations about ethics, but didn't you tell me your sister is engaged to the man who rescued her from that psycho that had all of you living under witness protection? You told me you love them being together and that he was good for her. Dustin was doing a job when he rescued her and it had nothing to do with the love that they felt for each other. I know what you do and I want to know more of who you are if you are willing to give it a chance."

"What if this ends badly?" she asked.

"I already know it won't. I can't tell you everything will be perfect, but I have come to appreciate life much more after what I've been through and I never want to take anything for granted again, especially a beautiful woman."

"You seem pretty sure of yourself."

"I'm sure about us and what I think we could have. I'm not shy when it comes to my feelings and the fact that I've been falling for you for weeks, months."

"So, what now?" Ava asked.

Calvin moved in closer until their bodies were flush up against each other, raising her arms up until they circled his neck. He then pulled her as close as he could to his body.

"Well, first, I think we should seal our newfound friendship with a kiss and this time, I'm hoping you won't run out of here like a bat out of hell like you did the last time. Maybe even stick around and have dinner with me?" he asked.

He didn't know if Ava had planned on responding or not because before she had a chance to, he leaned down and captured her lips. Like before, the passion between them grew quickly. What started out as a sweet kiss on the lips turned wild and salacious. Kissing her could be equal to the impact of a powerful drug.

Calvin moaned as they dueled for control of the

kiss, no longer thinking about any barriers, but going all in. Not caring about anything else but the feel and taste of her, he reached down and gathered Ava up until her legs circled his waist. Not sure he would be able to hold them up, not due to his leg, but due to the desire flowing through him that was making him weak in the knees, he walked until Ava's back rested against the closest wall, never breaking the kiss.

"No running this time?" he asked in between kissing her lips and finding the perfect spot on her neck to plant soft open-mouthed kisses.

"No running," Ava said.

"More?" he asked.

Breathlessly, Ava replied, "yes, more."

Inwardly, Calvin smiled, hoping this was the start of something wonderful between them. Turning with her in his arms, he headed for the elevator.

CHAPTER EIGHTEEN

Calvin exited the elevator on the bedroom level and walked with steady steps across the dark brown hardwood floor of the hallway, holding Ava in his arms with her legs wrapped securely around his waist. As he reached the doorway, he stopped to kick off his sneakers before he reached the deep burgundy carpeted floor of his bedroom. He kept his eyes on her going from her eyes down to her plump, thoroughly kissed lips. The passion growing between them was too much to leave alone and as his heart beat loudly in his chest, he gave silent thanks that she wanted him as much as he wanted her.

He and Ava had been dancing around their mutual attraction for weeks and putting the client/therapist business aside, he wanted her without any doubt.

Over the months as his therapist, he found her to be exactly what he would want in a woman long-term. She loved family as he did and the way she interacted with Camico warmed his heart. She was consoling and caring and not just from a professional perspective. He could feel the passion she was filled with and what he loved most was how she focused on listening when he had something weighing on his spirit. Though he could tell she was developing feelings for him by the way they interacted, she never shied away from anytime he wanted to talk about Sofia and what she meant to him. She understood and sympathized with his loss without jealousy. She was a woman he could see himself with. While he was in the military, he never thought he'd ever really settle down. Ava made him want to.

Walking toward the bed, the only sound in the room was that of the rain that beat and cascaded down the four large windows that lined the longest wall in the room.

"How are your legs?" Ava asked the minute they reached the bed and Calvin sat her on the edge where her legs dangled as the bed sat high off the floor.

Calvin smiled hoping he could get her to take off her business hat for a while.

"My legs are fine and I don't want you worrying about that. The only thing I want you concerned about is feeling. As much as I want you, I'm not going to compromise the progress we've made with my legs. I have more pressing needs at the moment," he admitted.

Ava shivered at the calming, soothing and loving sound of Calvin's deep, seductive baritone voice. The sound of it was doing delicious things to her.

"Has anyone ever told you that the sound of your voice is very erotic?" Ava asked.

"Yes, and if it's having an amatory impact on you, I'll talk all night long."

"All night long?" she said excitedly. "Your leg," she added.

"Well, if I have any problems with my leg, then we'll let you be in control, so yes, all night long," Calvin said and joined her on the bed.

Any words Ava could have thought to utter were locked in her throat as her eyes locked with Calvin's and the desire she saw in them was intense and overpowering. She could read every morsel of desire he had for her in the gleam of his eyes.

For months, she tried to deny what she was feeling for the handsome soldier who was placed in her care. Never had she ever felt the prevailing tug of her heart strings, not only for a client, but for any man. Calvin was strong and wore his heart on his sleeve like a badge of honor. She loved that about him and now, she was in bed with him about to satisfy the yearning that she'd been struggling with that she could no longer fight.

As they continued kissing, she could feel his hands all over her, pulling and tugging at her clothes hoping they would give way. Reaching down, as anxious as he was, she helped him divest her of every stitch of her clothing and then they turned to his. When they were naked, she was thankful the daylight that allowed her to see his perfectly sculpted body. If she thought he was a magnificent specimen with clothes on, she was blown away with lust at the sight of him in all of his glory and he was a sight to see.

"You look amazing," she admitted.

Calvin smiled, happy she liked what she saw.

"I want you to know even though we're naked and this may not be the time to bring this up, but this, what we're about to do, is not all I want from you. Don't get me wrong, I have dreamed about making love to you, but I want you, all of you. My interest in you is not about sex, though I'd be lying if I said I didn't want this," he said running his hand gently across the swell of her hips to indicate what he meant.

"Are you sure about that? My feelings wouldn't be hurt if your interest in me was purely sexual, though I would be disappointed," Ava said and leaned forward, placing a kiss on his muscled chest. When Calvin inhaled and held it in, her body tingled at his reaction to her.

"Baby, me wanting you intimately is a given, but I meant it when I said that's not all. I don't want to waste any time playing around when I can have an incredible woman like you. I want everything with you – dates, dinner, quiet nights watching old movies. You mean a lot to me and I want to show you how much in and out of the bedroom," Calvin admitted.

"Well, now that I'm here and getting my fill of you like this, I'm all about the sex right now," Ava laughed and punched his shoulder lightly to express her humor. She loved that she felt comfortable in his presence to joke even when they were naked.

"I'm here to please," Calvin said and rolled so that Ava was under him as he straddled her body, pressing his already hard member into the apex of her thighs. The moment Ava opened her legs wide to accommodate his body, he wasn't sure he would be able to last long once he was inside of her. He hadn't expected to be here with her like this now, but he knew it was exactly where he wanted to be – in her arms, about to love her like a woman should be loved, cherished and honored in the most intimate way.

"You are incredibly sexy. Thank you for trusting me when I say I don't want any hang-ups about what we are to each other. If you intend to back pedal, do it now because after we make love, I don't intend to go backwards or even forward without you. I want it all like I said," Calvin said, laying it all out for her.

"I'm not going anywhere that doesn't include you and Camico," she said. For once in her life, Ava was going to go with the flow and get what she wanted. She'd waited a long time to have a man she could trust and be herself around. Calvin was that man.

When he leaned down to kiss her, she reached between them to grasp his long, thick member as it stood at attention, pointing straight at her. It had been quite a few years since she'd last made love with a man, yet in the times that she had, she'd never been with a man whose penis was as long, thick and wide as Calvin's. Her mouth moistened at the thought of how powerfully strong and virile he looked above her. As they passionately kissed again, this time the kiss turned wild with an intensity that sent burning embers of desire to all points on her body.

As Calvin moved his hips in a circular motion while his penis poked around familiarizing her with the feel of him, she went with him as he rolled so that she was on top. This position made her feel empowered and the tigress in her made an appearance. She was about to straddle his hips like he had done her when she felt her body being lifted higher and higher up his body until her moistened center glided up to his lips. As she looked down at Calvin, knowing what he had in mind, she tried to prepare herself for what was next and soon learned, there was no way she could.

A swift swipe across her womanhood heightened her desire for him as he made love to her with his mouth. This wasn't a slow or unhurried act, but one that was penetrating and concentrated on giving her the best pleasure of her life. Without much forced movement, her hips moved with a desire of their own to get more and more from his mouth. This act wasn't one that she had a lot of experience with, but Calvin was definitely a master at it as his hands grabbed a hold of her hips, guiding her in a circular motion to be sure his tongue was giving her the ultimate pleasure.

"Ohhhhh!" she shouted and leaned forward until her palms rested on the bed above Calvin's head.

As he lapped at her, she tried to hold on through the best pleasure she'd ever gotten, but her body couldn't handle the intense sensation and without any pretense, she screamed as her release surged through her, electrifying the air around her. Her body moved uncontrollably as Calvin made sure his hands kept her in place. She could feel herself weakening while at the same time, invigorating her with the strength to run a mile without needing a break.

As her body calmed and she struggled to catch her breath, Calvin pulled her back down his body until her center rested against his rock-hard penis. The sensation of her stimulated labia rubbing against him once again had her body rising to the occasion. Calvin did promise her all night.

When they were eye-level with each other, she saw the smile on Calvin's face that said he was pleased with himself. She was pleased with him, too. Her body had never felt this good before.

"You taste amazing. I love how you react to me,"

he said.

"Mmm, you make it easy. That was incredible. I think I actually saw stars and I was sure I was transported temporarily to another dimension," she said leaning down to kiss him sweetly.

"In that case, let's see if we can get you on that transport again," he said while reaching into the stand next to the bed to retrieve protection.

As they kissed while he rolled it on, Calvin's hands shook with a keen desire to swiftly get inside of her. When he attempted to switch positions with Ava, she stopped him.

"Let me," she said.

Calvin opened his arms and placed his hands on the bed.

"Do you, baby," he said.

Ava did just that. She did her while at the same time, looking forward to doing him.

Raising her hips, Ava held her breath as she positioned her womanhood over the large, hard tip of him and slid down slowly, feeling her body swell to accommodate his large size. The feeling was the most powerful and amorous sensation she'd ever experienced. The feeling was so great, she had a hard time focusing as she felt his hardness press up into her easing in and out slowly.

Calvin couldn't see it, but he could feel his teeth grinding as Ava loomed over him moving like a she-devil, staking her claim on him. He was already on the brink, but was determined to hold off in order to be sure Ava got every bit of pleasure from their coupling that she wanted and needed.

Grabbing on to her hips again, he held on as she rode him as their moans filled the air in the room. As his body moved into her with long, expansive strokes, Calvin raised his legs, bending them at the knee in order to brace himself for more powerful surges into her body. Reaching for her hands, he linked their fingers above his head as the pace increased as he glided in and out of her womanhood.

"You feel so good, Ava!" Calvin huffed out as he continued to furrow up with powerful strokes. He was glad he was holding Ava's hands or she surely would have fallen off of him as their lovemaking turned wild. The wet slippery sounds cascading in the room drove his passion for her higher and higher and when she screamed that her orgasm was imminent, he was right there with her.

"Let go, sweetness," he uttered.

Ava knew the only option for her was to let go and she did. A streak of white lights flashed across her eyes as she threw her head back and let a mind-blowing release shatter her into a million pieces. She could feel Calvin throbbing inside of her and that sensation sent her higher and higher until she felt like she was floating on air. She was having the best out of body experience and she never wanted to come down. She moved and rode and let her body lead her to ecstasy.

Calvin was done trying to hold on as a penetrating feeling seared through him and he joined Ava in his very own powerful orgasm. His body exploded again and again as his hips bucked ferociously under her like a wild animal. He moved in and out of her until his body became to calm as Ava's did and they collapsed in a heap of sated bliss. He wasn't even sure he was still alive.

As Ava laid her body completely on his, Calvin could feel the slipperiness from the sweat that covered their bodies as his arms encircled her body, keeping them intimately connected. He had to force his body to calm even more while at the same time, working to control his breaths in and out.

"I'm not sure I can move," Ava said softly in his ear.

"You don't have to move. You feel good just like this."

"Did that just happen? I swear I think my soul left my physical body for a few minutes there. I've never experienced anything that intense before in my life," she said.

"I'm with you on that. I may have to re-think my all-night idea. I'm not sure I'll survive a full night of what you just put on me. I may never let you out of this bed," Calvin quipped.

Ava leaned up and found his lips with hers. She never wanted to lose the connection they were sharing. She knew being with him would be good, but what she'd just experienced couldn't be measured.

"Well, you promised me all-night and after what you just dished out, I'm holding you to that. I don't have anyplace to be," she joked.

"That's good to know because after I get us some sustenance, I'm going to need a repeat."

"You're on!" she yelled and leaned back down as Calvin fully embraced her against him.

"Just so that we are clear, this isn't something casual or some one-time thing. I admit I wasn't planning on this happening today, but I'm glad it did and when I said I want more than just your body, I meant it. I hope you can see us spending more time together like this and out of bed and I don't want any talk of ethics," he said.

Ava chuckled. She'd already forgotten the fact that he was her client. They were far beyond that now.

"No ethics talk and I'd like more, too. I don't know where this thing between us will lead, but I'm open to exploring it. For one minute though, let me put my work hat on and I promise I won't do it again," Ava pleaded with words and with her eyes.

Calvin knew the moment she looked at him, he would never deny her anything.

"Just this once," he said.

"How is your leg? You were pretty acrobatic. Any pain right now?" she asked.

"No pain at all and I would be honest and tell you if there was. Now, what about you? Any pain?

You know what I mean," he said letting her know that his mind wasn't far from the fact that he was larger than any guy she'd ever been with and with her tightness, she may be experiencing a little discomfort.

"A little, but not much. That has to do with the fact that as I mentioned, I haven't done this in a long time."

Calvin laughed.

"I couldn't tell. You took control and went all in," he quipped.

"You made it easy with how good you feel. Now, about that sustenance thing. I think you've helped me work up a serious appetite," she said.

Calvin rolled them over until she was flat on her back under him.

"You stay here and I'll get us some food and a bottle of wine," he said kissing her and then moving off of the bed.

Leaving the bed, Calvin went into the bathroom that was a part of his master suite and exposed of the condom. While in the room alone, he took a moment and thought about what they'd just experienced. Their coming together was fulfillment on a level he'd never experienced. He couldn't believe his heart was still beating after such intensity. Ava had helped bring him back to life not just through therapy, but through a connection he wasn't sure he'd ever find. He'd waited weeks for her to see that they were something special and they were. He was ready for more and it had nothing to do with sex.

CHAPTER NINETEEN

Valencio smiled as he walked into the meeting, where gathered around the table were men assembled to carry out the orders he was about to give them. He now had the information he had been waiting on. The Admiral had come through with the name of the man who had gotten his daughter pregnant and stolen his grandson away.

Gripping the papers tight in his hand, he sat at the head of the table.

"We're packing up and heading to Texas in a few days. As soon as I can get the particulars worked out, we're going to pay Calvin Lymon a visit," he said.

"Calvin Lymon?" one of the men questioned.

"Yes. He's the man I've been looking for. I have his name and I'm waiting on exact information on where in Texas he's located. My connect is going to send someone ahead to make sure he's there and that he has my grandson with him. I want to see photos or video of my grandson and then Calvin will pay for what he did to me," Valencio said as he spoke in a vile tone.

"What are our orders, sir?" another man asked.

Valencio looked around the table at the eight men who were assembled. He was unable to get any of the men who were still loyal to him in South America out of that country. He was able to get men who would do anything for money right from this country. If they did their job right, each would be set up for life and he would have his grandson back. No one stole from him without consequences.

"Your orders will be to go in and get my grandson without harming him in any way. If even one hair on his head is hurt, you're all dead and you may as well kill yourself. Camico is all I care about. Is that clear?" he asked.

All head shook in the affirmative as he looked around the table.

"When are we heading out?" one man asked.

"I'm waiting for confirmation and we'll be on our way. I'll be at a secluded location and I expect you to bring my grandson to me. I'd like this man who fathered him brought to me alive so that I can look him in the face when I snuff out his life, but if that's not possible, so be it. I want photos of his dead body and anyone else associated with him. I want him to feel what it's like to lose everyone important to him."

"What about our money?"

Valencio watched as each man lit up with questionable looks on their faces. He wasn't planning on telling them that he had no plans of paying them anywhere near the amount he'd promised. What he had already given them was all they were going to get. Once he had his grandson back in his arms, he would disappear and in South America where everyone feared him, no one would ever be able to get close enough to him, let alone these guys.

"Your money will be delivered the moment I have my grandson and our business will be done. You all received your advanced payments and the balance you'll see when I get Camico and Calvin Lymon. My grandson alive and Calvin, dead or alive. If he has family, I want them dead and for him to know that it was my order that you're carrying out. He's military, but he won't be expecting you. By now, I'm sure he thinks he's safe because it's been almost six months since he snatched Camico away. I want to catch him off-guard."

"When are we getting this additional intel?" someone asked.

"I should have it in a few days and then we'll be on our way. I would prefer taking cars and not flights. I can't have anything leading back to me until I'm back in South America. I don't want anyone on any radars. This has to be lowkey."

"You the man with the money, so it's whatever you say."

"Good. I've got some phone calls to make. I want

everyone ready to go at a moment's notice. It's time to put an end to this," Valencio said as he stood and walked out of the room.

He sneered when he thought of the room full of fools who trusted his every word. He has never been nor will he ever be a man of his word. All he wanted was his grandson and then he'd return to his stomping grounds where he'd already increased security around his new compound, one no one had yet to figure out belonged to him. It was where he planned to raise Camico to one day take over his operations.

"I'm getting close Calvin Lymon. I have a special bullet with your name on it," he said to no one as he went into the bedroom he'd been using since he entered the country. He had a few more plans to make and thank to his friend the Admiral, he would get out of the United States as easily as he had gotten into it.

~~

Ava moved around her kitchen checking pots, making sure everything was ready for Calvin and Camico's visit. They were planning a quiet evening at her place and she'd promised him one of her delicious home cooked meals. She was looking forward to a night with her two favorite people.

After their first intimate encounter two weeks ago, she and Calvin had fallen into a comfortable place in their relationship. His therapy sessions were done and she was happy that he was showing very little discomfort when using the leg that had suffered the most damage. He was back to working out regularly which included running. Already, he was up to running three miles a day. He was definitely on the mend in more than one way.

Once his life had gotten back to some normalcy, Callie had finally helped him plan a nice, quiet memorial for Sofia. Thankful for knowing the right people, Sofia's body was brought from South America to the United States and his family was able to have her buried at a cemetery that wasn't far from where he and Camico lived.

It sickened her to know that Valencio had made no arrangements for either of his children, leaving their care to extended family. Now, at least, she would be at a place where Calvin could take Camico to over the years. She was also happy to know that it seemed Calvin had gotten over being concerned about Valencio. He knew that every effort had been made to try and locate him and it appeared he had gone underground so deep that no one knew where he was. Perhaps, he had been injured so bad that he hadn't survived. Either way, he was prepared for any sudden movement out of South America that may target him.

Now that they were spending a lot of time together and at his house, he had shown her the various high-secure areas of his house that she needed to be aware of in case of an emergency. She'd never seen a panic room before or all of the equipment Calvin had built. One other thing he'd taken time to show her was how to protect herself and shoot a gun. She had always feared having a weapon in her hands, but she knew she needed to know how to protect herself. If she had known that many years ago, she may not have had to live a secret life for so many years.

A week ago, she actually had the chance to spend time with Calvin's family. She, like the rest of the world, had been fascinated by the likes of Cade Weston, but to her, he still didn't measure up to Calvin.

His family had gathered for a private showing of Cade's newest movie and from what she saw, it was going to be the next big hit.

After the movie, they celebrated with food and music and she got the chance to connect with his family on a personal level and not as Calvin's therapist. She loved that his family went out of their way to make her feel comfortable in her role as Calvin's girlfriend. The highlight of her time with them was being able to finally play with Colby and see how much Camico loved his little cousin.

Later that night as she lay in Calvin's arms after making love at his house while Camico slept soundly in his room, they talked about where their relationship was going. Though she was tired the next day, they ended up staying up all night talking in depth about their feelings for each other and what was next for them. They were on the same page knowing that their connection wasn't a fluke as client and therapist, but their mutual attraction was real and not just on a physical level. They shared more than just the basics of what they liked and did not like in life. She shared her inner most feelings about what she'd gone through living in California and hiding out. Calvin shared with her his reservations about going back to join his SEAL team.

Now that he had Camico, he wasn't so sure that he was ready to leave him. His life had changed a lot and not only was his doubt because of Camico, but also because of the strong feelings he had developed for her. For the first time in his life, there was something more important to him than the military. He admired the love Cade and Callie shared and could see himself in that kind of loving relationship with her and she was hopeful because she was in love with him. They hadn't shared words of love, but they had shared that they were loving the committed relationship they were having.

She had also shared that whatever choice he made about going back to being a SEAL, she would support him. Most important to her is his happiness. Wherever he chose to be, she would be in his corner.

Tonight was going to be another night like so many they'd been having lately. Thankful for her business partner, she was able to keep her appointments to daytime hours and then enjoy downtime with Calvin and Camico. He made a comment the other night that they were a family – the three of them. She loved how it felt. She was looking forward to hosting them, since usually they spent their time at Calvin's house so that Camico could be at home. If they stayed the night together at her place, it was because Camico was with Cade and Callie.

With things in the kitchen all set up, she checked her family room to be sure she'd set things up there as well. She smiled at the pile of toys that sat in the middle of the floor. She hadn't told Calvin she was going to pick up a few things for Camico to play with so that he felt comfortable at her place. There were soft block toys, trucks and large colorful rings. She'd also picked up a few books with big, bright pictures she knew he'd like. She'd also bought her own nephew, who was around Camico's age, the same toys when her brother, Vinnie came to visit a few months back with his girlfriend and baby son, Gino. She was glad she'd picked up a crib and a few other items for their visit and that he brother left them with her for their next visit. If Calvin wanted to put Camico down for a nap, she had a crib ready for him. She wanted them to be just as comfortable at her house as Calvin made he the many times she'd been to his house.

With everything in order and ready for their visit, she had a few minutes to sit and relax. Just as she sat down in front of the television, she was startled by the ringing of her cell phone. She smiled when she picked it up from the table and saw her sister's picture on the screen.

"Hey, Sis! What's shakin' with you?" Ava asked.

"Wait, did you just say shakin' without the 'g' at the end? You're in a good mood. What gives?" Nina asked.

"Nothing gives. I'm happy you called."

"Yeah, that's not it, so spill it."

"You called me for a reason. Why don't we start with that?" Ava asked. She was planning to tell her all about Calvin, but she needed to get her thoughts about it straight first. She wanted to shout to Nina that she was in love, but she hadn't even had that conversation with Calvin yet. Thinking about him made her heart flutter. Things were going so well, she had to pinch herself sometimes to be sure she was actually involved with that gorgeous man.

"Right. I called to say I may be coming to visit you in a few weeks. I want to be sure you're going to be there."

"You're coming for a visit? Well, it's about time. I miss you!" Ava shouted.

"I miss you, too. I know Vinnie was there with the baby a few months ago. I want to visit him soon, too. Pretty soon, I won't be able to fly and I want to see you sooner rather than later," Nina said.

Ava smiled and then her frown turned into a frown.

"What's wrong? Why won't you be able to fly

soon?"

She could almost hear Nina smiling through the phone.

"You're pregnant?"

"Yes!" Nina shouted.

Ava jumped up from the chair and bounced up and down. Nothing could make her happier than to know Nina was having a baby, a sign that she was finally happy. Then again, who wouldn't be happy with a man like Dustin, her knight in shining armor. He'd shown her the way a woman should be treated and after the kind of men her sister had a habit of connecting with, Dustin was a relief.

"Congratulations! How happy is Dustin?" she asked.

"He is ecstatic! He never had a lot of family other than his military family. He's looking forward to having his own child. I want some time with you before the baby is born."

"Of course, you know I'll coming out to California when the baby is born."

"Yes! I didn't want to ask because I know you're getting your company up and running and you spend every waking hour working."

Ava smiled as her thoughts turned to Calvin.

"Not every hour, but some," she admitted.

"Only some? Okay, so now your time to spill it."

Ava sat back down and tried not to freak out while telling Nina about the man in her life.

"I'm seeing someone and it's amazing being

involved with him. He's sexy, considerate and I feel good around him. In fact, I'm waiting on him and his son to come over tonight for dinner," she said.

"He has a son?" Nina asked.

"Yes. He's a single father raising his son named Camico and let me tell you that little boy of his has already stolen my heart."

"Who is this man?"

This is where Ava's nerves became unsettled. She once said she didn't mix business with pleasure, yet that's what she did with Calvin and she had no regrets.

"Do you remember the client Trey wanted to refer to me here in Texas?"

"The military guy that was injured?" Nina asked.

"Yes. His name is Calvin Lymon and we've been seeing each other for several weeks now."

"You go sis! He's the fine one. So, out the door went your mantra that you don't mix work with pleasure? For the record, I'm not judging. I told you to go for it and stop worry about some line you thought you couldn't cross. I can tell you're happy."

"Nina, I have never been this happy before. Calvin is absolutely amazing and you should see him with his son."

"How serious is this? Am I hearing love in your voice?"

Ava bit her bottom lip and wondered if she should share that before she had actually said it out loud to Calvin. Nina was her sister in whom she could share anything.

"Yes. I'm in love with him, but I haven't told him yet. We've been enjoying a great relationship and haven't talked about deep feelings. He suffered a huge loss when Camico's mother died and I'm not sure he's ready to hear the love word from another woman right now."

"Don't cut yourself short. You're just as amazing as he is and he's lucky to have you and to have your love. You know what we went through and how our lives were for a few years. It's taught you, Vinnie and me to appreciate life and love a little more. I'm sure if he's been through something major like the loss of his son's mother, he also would appreciate life even more, especially if you're in love with each other."

"I don't know if he's in love with me," Ava said nervously.

"Of course, he is. No man can be around you and not love you. I look forward to meeting him when I visit."

"You're really going to like him," Ava said, happily.

"I'm going to let you go to get ready for him. I'll call you in a few days to talk about a week to visit. I wanted to call and say hello since I can do that any time now that we're not living undercover anymore. I love you, sis. I'm happy you're happy!" Nina said.

"I love you, too and I'm glad you, Vinnie and I are living our best life."

"That we are."

"Love you!" Ava said.

"Love you more!" Nina replied.

After she hung up, Ava checked the time and rushed around knowing that Calvin would soon be on his way.

Using the remote to turn on some music, she sang to the sounds of Ledisi that flooded the room with her mystical voice. She was in a great mood and she was in love.

CHAPTER TWENTY

"Calvin, we have a problem."

His spine stiffened as he listened to the worried tone of Mason's voice. He had just finished chasing Camico around to keep him still long enough to get clothes on him as they prepared to head to Ava's place for dinner. Just as he was about to head out to the car after packing Camico's bag, his cell phone rang. He was happy to hear from Mason, but then an ice-cold feeling shot through his bones, knowing whatever Mason was going to say, it wasn't going to be good.

Picking Camico up in his arms, he went into SEAL mode and checked the camera's the showed the perimeter of his property. Even though he was a new father, his protective mode set in as he kept Camico close. He knew where his weapons were and was prepared to head to the panic room he'd had built if it meant he had to protect his son's life.

"What's going on?" he said.

"Valencio has surfaced. Where I'm not sure, but

he's surfaced. Also, our hunch that he was getting help from someone in this country turned out to be true. Some very reputable sources confirmed that there is a major leak in military activities and that someone leaked the names of every SEAL member. I don't think they were able to pinpoint you specifically, but there is a chance, Valencio's money is reaching across the ocean and he's trying to find Camico."

"Damn!" Calvin said so loud and harsh, he startled Camico who looked at him wide-eyed with fright. To ease the fear on his son's face, he smiled and nuzzled his neck. Camico loved that and his frown turned to a huge smile as he giggled.

"Is that my godson I hear?" Mason said.

"Yes, we were on our way to Ava's house for dinner."

"Look at you being all domesticated," Mason said. "I bet you don't even miss the team," he added.

"Not when it comes to comparing life with the team to life with my son. Camico will win every time," he said.

"Does that mean you're not coming back even after you're cleared for duty whenever that is?"

"I don't know yet. I've made provisions for Camico to live with Cade and Callie if I decide to go back, but I'm having reservations, especially if Valencio is out there somewhere. I can't protect Camico if I'm not here."

"Dude, with the security Cade has around at all times, you have nothing to worry about and that house of yours is a mini fortress inside. I do understand what you mean. That little guy has already lost his mother and doesn't need to be away from you, too."

"That's all I'm saying. I have a lot to think about and then there's Ava. I love her and I never thought this would be me, but I love the way we've settled into this loving relationship, this feeling of family with her and Camico. I understand how easy it was for Cade to give up his playboy ways and settle into husband and father mode."

"I'm happy for you. I know what losing Sofia meant to you. I'm glad you were able to find love with Ava. I want you to do what you need to do on your end and on my end, I'm going to continue to dig into Valencio's whereabouts. I do have some bad news that could mean and even worse scenario for you."

Calvin braced himself for what was next.

"Hit me with it," he said and waited.

"Pierre is dead."

"Pierre?" he asked and thought hard about where he knew that name from.

"Yes, he was a friend of Sofia's. He was the guy who helped protect Camico before I was able to get him out of the country."

"Was it Valencio?" Calvin asked, but knew the answer before Mason spoke it.

"Yes. He was tortured and I won't share those details with you. It appears he tried to get information about you out of him."

"Damn. He didn't know anything about me – not enough that would be of any help to Valencio. What about Antonia? She was Sofia's best friend and she knows everything that Sofia knew about me. Is she safe and if not, can we get her to safety?" Calvin asked. He was deeply concerned about her. She was instrumental in helping Sofia get away to be with him.

"From what I was able to find out, Sofia had been filtering money to Antonia to hide for her for years. After Sofia died, Antonia disappeared, no doubt taking that money and starting a new life for her and her mother, the only family that she really had. Valencio wasn't able to get to her. If he had, he would already be at your door."

Calvin breathed a sigh of relief. He was happy knowing Antonia didn't suffer because of how she helped him and Sofia.

"Okay, what else do you know? What about this help Valencio is getting? Any idea who it is?"

When Mason kept quiet and didn't answer, Calvin knew the answer must be someone who knew he was the man Valencio was looking for.

"There is an Admiral that we believe is the leak and on Valencio's payroll. I'm flying to a secluded spot in Seattle, Washington tomorrow morning where the Admiral is currently attending a summit.

I don't care how high up the food chain this guy is, if he's compromised you and this country in any way by taking bribes from Valencio and his cartel, he'll have hell to pay. The least of his worries will be a court martial for treason. I'll keep you posted. For now, I wanted you to know to watch your back. There is still a chance Valencio knows nothing. It's been months with no sightings or word of him. I think he's back to old business and letting go of ever getting Camico back since he doesn't know where he is. Keep your ears on just in case we need to go stealth with our communication. I'm not sure how deep the rabbit hole goes with the information leak. I've got your back. Our whole team has your back. I even talked to Trey and Dustin out of California. I've updated them and they've agreed to use their company if our military chooses to not get involved in this personal matter. Trey is heading to Texas tomorrow, so be on the lookout for him."

"Great. I was expecting a visit from him soon. He wants to talk to me about options if I choose not to return to active duty. They are interested in starting a Texas branch of their Game Changers security and protection services and they want me to run it. I'm actually considering it. Though I'll have missions that will take me away sometimes, for the most part, I'll be right here in Texas and near my son."

"Dada, Dada, Dada" Camico said as he tried unsuccessfully to get down to run around.

"Sounds like he wants your attention. You go ahead and try to enjoy your evening with Ava. Tell her I said hello and kiss Camico for me. I will be in Texas to visit soon. My priority is making sure Valencio is no longer a threat."

"Okay, but I don't want you facing this by yourself," Calvin said.

"Bro, the entire team is behind me on this. I wasn't able to get permission to tackle this through the military, but nothing is stopping me from handling this guy if need be and our brothers are on board one hundred percent. You know I'll always have your back," Mason said.

"I know and it means everything. Keep me posted and thanks for reminding me that the threat is still out there."

Calvin disconnected the call, grabbed Camico's bag and headed into the garage. He needed to keep his routine night in play because he didn't want to worry Ava, but in the back of his mind, he knew Valencio would forever be a threat as long as he was alive. If Valencio planned to step foot into his world, he was going to make sure he didn't survive this time.

After putting Camico in his car seat and handing him his favorite black and orange stuffed giraffe, he exited the garage and secured the elaborate house alarm system by using his phone and headed to Ava's house. Like Mason said, he would make sure to watch his own back and any signs that someone was watching him.

~~

Ava rushed to her condo door to let Calvin and Camico in. She had promised him an Italian spaghetti dinner from scratch the way her mother had taught her to make. When she opened the door, her heart fluttered seeing Calvin standing there with a smile on his face that said he was just as happy to see her as she was to see him. Her heart sped up when he leaned down and kissed her softly on the lips.

"Hey good lookin'," Calvin said as Camico bounced around in his arms reaching for Ava.

"Hey yourself," she said, making funny faces at Camico who laughed so hard his whole body shook.

"Looks like my son wants all of your attention tonight. I guess I'll have to fight him for the top spot," Calvin chuckled as he handed a now fussy Camico to her.

"He can get as much attention from me as he wants," she said nuzzling Camico who laughed uncontrollably.

"Something smells good."

"That would be the perfect Italian dinner I'm cooking. I even picked up a few chicken nuggets to pop in the oven for Camico along with apple sauce, something you said was his favorite."

Calvin smiled. Could he have met a more perfect woman? Not one more perfect than Ava, he thought.

"You thought of everything," he said.

"I did and that includes a few toys for this little guy here."

Ava walked toward the family room right off of the kitchen and the minute Camico saw all of the colorful toys, he wanted to get down. The minute he hit the floor, he raced for the toys, falling twice. Before either of them could help him up, he found his footing and sat down in front of the pile.

"What's all that?" Calvin asked, smiling at how happy Camico was. To the floor and out of the way went the stuffed giraffe.

"Just a few things I picked up for Camico's first visit to my house."

"You know you didn't have to do that."

"I know, but I wanted to. Was that okay?" Ava asked.

"Yes, perfect. Look how happy he is."

"You keep an eye on him while I get dinner ready."

Before she could get too far away, Calvin turned her for a more passionate kiss than the one they shared at the door. The moment his lips touched hers, she sighed with relief and how much she'd missed the connection with him even though it had only been a few days since she'd last saw him.

The kiss was over quickly and for now, she accepted that because Camico was the priority. She hoped that Calvin planned to remedy that before the night was over.

"I needed that," Calvin said as he kept his eye on Camico while letting her know how much he needed to feel close to her.

Ava saw something in Calvin's eyes that bothered her. Something was wrong and he was trying to hide it. They had spent enough time together that she could read the signs when something was on his mind.

"Are you okay?" she asked.

"We'll talk about it later."

Kissing her quickly on the cheek, Calvin walked over and sat on the floor to play with Camico. On his mind was the fact that Valencio may be getting close to finding out who he was. The one consolation is that with Valencio on the most wanted list, he wouldn't be able to get into the country without setting off warnings. For that he was grateful, but that didn't mean he didn't still have connections he could send after Camico if he obtained information on them. He had to assume trouble was coming. He wouldn't live in seclusion and hoped Mason could get information soon on what Valencio knew.

"I talked to my sister a little while ago. She's coming to town for a visit soon and I think Dustin is coming with her."

"Really? I know you're happy about that. I'm sure you've missed each other."

"You have no idea. My brother was here for a visit and I hated when he had to leave."

"Trey is coming to town in two weeks. Maybe Dustin is coming with him then."

"He is?"

"He and Dustin are talking to me about starting up a new division of their company here in Texas and they want me to run it if by chance I'm thinking of not going back and Trey is coming to lay everything out for me. He also has some new weapons and equipment he wants me to check out."

"You're thinking about it? About not going back?" Ava asked.

She didn't want to sway him one way or the other and knew he was struggling with leaving Camico."

"It's something that's been on my mind."

"I can see it's not the only thing on your mind, but like you said we'll talk about that later. You know I'm here for you and anytime you need an ear to just listen, you will have my undivided attention."

Calvin turned around and looked over the high-back of the sofa, stretching his neck to see her from his position on the floor.

"I appreciate that and I appreciate you. I can't begin to tell you what you've come to mean to me."

"As long as you know I'm here for you. Now, get that little guy and let's eat. I'll pop his nuggets in a pan in the oven and they'll only take a few minutes. For now, his applesauce is here on the counter. I'm setting our foot out now," she said.

"You're so good to me."

Ava smiled. She was happy that she could make him happy.

CHAPTER TWENTY-ONE

Calvin was distracted. As much as he was enjoying his evening with Ava and there was no doubt Camico was having a good time, he couldn't take his mind off of his conversation with Mason.

Though he was up and moving around, pretty much back to normal, he still hadn't been cleared by his doctor to return to duty and he knew if he could go back just to capture Valencio, he would do that. He had to protect his family.

When he thought about family, he looked at Camico who sat in Ava's lap, a lot quieter than he had been. He knew it was getting close to his bed time. His family was right in front of him. Of course, he had Cade and his family, Cameron and his grandparents, but now, he had Camico and Ava to think about. Yes, she was now his family, too.

He loved how comfortably they felt as a family. Still, he was having a hard time staying focused when he knew that a threat lingered outside the walls of this country. How much longer would it be before the connection is made to him and thereby exposing Camico to the danger that is his grandfather? If Valencio was able to get to Pierre, there was no telling how much he learned.

The television played before them, but no one was watching it. He was thinking hard and Ava was giving Camico the attention he needed from her until he rubbed his eyes, a sign he was tired and ready for sleep.

Calvin smiled brightly when Camico reached for him, wanting to be in his lap.

"I think he's winding down," Ava said as Camico yarned and laid his head on Calvin's chest. When he began to move around restlessly, Calvin knew within seconds, Camico would take the roof off the place with his screams for a bottle. He'll be grumpy when he sees that the only means of getting milk was through a sippy cup.

He'd been trying to get Camico off of a bottle since he turned a year old and slowly he was working up to it. Luckily, at night, his little ball of fire didn't put up much fuss when he saw the cup instead of a bottle

"I agree and in a minute, we'll both get to hear his siren. I need to get his cup ready," Calvin said and tried to stand. The moment he moved, Camico whimpered.

"Don't move. I'll get it. If you move, he'll explode," she quipped.

Doing everything he could to distract Camico

from funny faces to crazy noises, Calvin wanted to give Ava time to get the cup of milk. Within seconds, Camico started bouncing around when he saw the cup in Ava's hands. The minute she handed it to him, he put the cup to his lips and leaned back into the crook of Calvin's arms where he sipped until he quickly fell back asleep.

This, Calvin thought is what his entire world was about. His son and the woman he loved. As they quieted down so that Camico would fall asleep, he embraced Ava when she leaned over and snuggled against him while putting her feet under her on the sofa.

Reaching for the remote, he turned the volume down and pulled Camico and Ava closer into his embrace. He never wanted to be away from them for long periods of time. He already knew his decision was pretty much made for him. He would not be returning to his team. Life was short and he wanted to make the best of it and what was best was to be with his family.

To his wonder, as he lifted Camico to his shoulder where he could more comfortably lay his head now that he was asleep, he felt Ava, who leaned her head on his other shoulder, had fallen asleep.

Silently, he pledged to protect his family no matter what, even if it meant his life. He knew Camico would be taken care of if anything happened to him. Holding his two loves so close to his body, he felt like he could feel one heart beating for the three of them, tying them together.

This is what Cade is always telling him about. He said when the moment that he really took stock of his life and what it was meant to be, he would know what his next move should be when it came to whether he goes into business with his friends or risk distancing himself from his only son.

He had been struggling with the idea of going back to join his SEAL team or work with Trey on opening up a Texas branch of his security and investigation company and staying close to raise his son and now to also love Ava. How many times does love come around in a lifetime?

An hour later, he was still having the same thoughts, unable to rest or even relax. The hour was late, a little after eleven at night and he had never felt more content in his entire life. He had a woman he loved and his son in his arms and this is how he could protect them, especially knowing that a threat still existed. Valencio was still out there somewhere and until he that was no longer the case, he had to assume that at any time, he'd be found and therefore, that meant that Camico would be found.

The thought of that man had him holding Camico and Ava a little tighter to him, causing Ava to stir.

"I'm sorry, I didn't mean to wake you," he said.

Ava came awake and looked over at Camico first before looking up into the beautiful yet, worrisome eyes of Calvin.

"What time is it? I didn't realize I had fallen asleep. You can't be comfortable with both of us smothering you," she said and tried to move away. Calvin continued to hold her close.

"I could never hold you and my son close enough. It's a little after eleven. You and Camico have been knocked out for a while."

"You've been sitting here like a statue trying not to wake us?" she quipped.

Calvin laughed quietly, trying not to move with Camico on his shoulder. With any luck, he was now asleep for the night.

"I have been and loving every minute of it," he said leaning down and placing a soft kiss on her forehead.

"What's that look in your eyes? I've seen it all evening long. I actually saw it the night a few weeks ago at Camico's birthday party. Are you going to tell me what's going on? What has you so worried?"

Calvin thought back to that day and the fun they had as a family. After Callie hired the best event planner on the planet, they had a Disney Land themed party. With Callie and her family being from the area, she had invited longtime friends and family, his grandparents had come to town, Cade was in town taking some much-needed time off and even Cameron had come home for the event. That day had been as close to perfect as perfect could be, but in the back of his mind, he couldn't stop thinking of being found out.

The work he had done on his house was good, but it wasn't great. He didn't want his house to be a fortress like the kind of compound Valencio had lived in, but he needed to secure it for his son's safety. Now that the inside was more secure than the White House, he needed to focus on the open grounds surrounding the property.

He leaned down and kissed Ava again before responding.

"I have this feeling that I should be worried and I can't shake it. I know for months, I've been focused on my recovery and taking advantage of this time with family, but as long as Valencio is alive, my son isn't safe," he admitted.

"I thought Valencio didn't know your true identity?"

"I thought that also, but I'm not so sure. He has a way of getting information and I wouldn't put it past him to have U.S. connections."

"Did anyone besides Sofia know your true identity?" Ava asked.

"A few people and I'm worried Valencio will use any tactic to get that information from them whether he believes them when they say they have no idea who I really am. He killed someone that was close to Sofia to try and get information. I don't think he got it. There is also her best friend who I think was actually able to get away. The only people left are the two women who helped take care of

Camico. I don't know what happened to them."

"I thought efforts were still in place to locate him?"

"That's the thing – I know he's still out there, but he's hiding and getting help. Money speaks and he's got lots of it even after all that was seized. What was recovered only scratched the surface when it comes to the millions he has. He could buy a lot of help with that."

"I know you're concerned and I understand why, but you're going to worry yourself about something you can't do anything about right now."

"If I were a part of the search team..." Calvin said, but didn't finish.

"I know. If you were, he wouldn't be a threat anymore. Again, you can't worry forever. I've spent enough nights with you to know that you don't sleep well and that concerns me."

"Every time I close my eyes, all I see is Camico screaming for me as Valencio carries him away. I can't let that become a reality. I can't have my son under armored guard every day. That's no kind of life for him. That's the kind of life Valencio would have for him and I don't want that. His mother didn't want that and with my last breath, I will protect him."

Ava sat up straight and turned Calvin's face toward hers.

"You are doing everything you can to protect him and anyone can see your son adores you. He is here now with you because you did what you needed to do to make that happen. There are so many people in your court to help you love and care for him that even if Valencio found out who you were, he wouldn't dare risk your wrath by coming after your son. I bet he's someplace living underground and possibly giving up on the idea of trying to locate Camico without any leads."

"I hope you're right, for his sake," Calvin said and grimaced at the thought.

Ava saw more worry lines across his handsome face and wanted to find a way to relax him.

Calvin smiled at her and she hoped that she was being as much support to him as he has been to her when she told him about her past and what she and her siblings went through at the hands of a crazy, madman. She understood Calvin's reservations because she had thought that she was untouchable.

"Let's put Camico down. My brother was here recently with his son and I purchased a crib and some other baby things for his son who is a little younger than Camico. Let me put some clean sheets on the crib mattress and let him really stretch out," she offered.

"We don't want to put you out," Calvin said.

"That's crazy. After all of the times I've stayed at your house, I think the idea of the two of you spending the night here is fine. I promise all the doors and windows are securely locked," she said smiling and standing up.

Calvin stood and followed her into one of the bedrooms. Inside it was a regular bed, dresser and in the corner was a brown wood crib. He held and rocked Camico until she had everything ready. When he laid him down, he waited to see if he would wake up, but he didn't.

Ava searched around in the closet for the baby monitor and locating it, she plugged one end in and carried the other with them back out into the main room, pulling the door behind them.

"Are you sure you're good with this? It's not too late and Camico and I can get out of your hair."

"I want you both here. Now, as for you, lets lighten your mood. I want to dance," Ava said.

"Dance?"

"Yes, dance. You look worried all the time like your mind is always planning and tonight, all I want you to do is relax with no worries of bad men coming to snatch your son away. You won't let that happen and neither will I."

Ava turned the television off and reached for the remote to the sound bar. Setting her phone up to the music application, she started swaying the moment she heard her favorite New Edition song.

"New Edition? Really?"

"Yes! I know it's old school, but I love them."

"I do, too," Calvin admitted.

"Good, then start moving!"

As they danced, Calvin realized he did feel better. He cleared his mind of everything except her, the most beautiful woman in the world to him. No words were needed as they moved together and apart while still in sync.

As they danced around the room, Calvin began to feel better as he was able to focus on her and him. After a few minutes, the song changed and a slower one played throughout the room.

"Come here," Calvin said drawing Ava into his arms.

"My favorite place to be is in your arms," she said hugging him tighter.

"You are an amazing woman. I want you to know that. I have loved every second we've spent together even when you were dishing out orders during my therapy. That time has led me here and I'm thankful. Being with you has been surprising, not because I had any question about what we could be together, but because I wasn't expecting to fall in love with you, but I have. I love you, Ava and you and Camico are what make my world go around. This love isn't about making love or anything we can touch and feel," he said.

Calvin reached for Ava's hand and placed it over his heart.

"I can feel how hard your heart is beating," she said.

"I know. My heartbeat is you and my son. It's filled with love for you both like nothing I've ever experienced before. I won't survive if anything happens to either one of you."

Ava reached up and caressed Calvin's face. She wanted him to feel loved and secure knowing he didn't have to carry the weight of wondering if Valencio would one day come, all by himself. She was along for the full ride and as long as he wanted her, she was looking at forever.

"I love you, too. I love you so much and it hurts me to see you worry as much as you do. Let me be here for you and provide you with that safe place to forget about everything in the world except for you, me and Camico."

"We're in love," he uttered before leaning down and stroking her lips with his. He needed to feel the connection to her and know that even if it's only for a short while, nothing could penetrate the happy moment.

"Yes, we are and that love is what will keep your heart beating. Nothing is going to happen to me or Camico and definitely not you because Valencio has no idea who he is up against. If he is a threat, he will be dealt with."

Calvin grinned. This woman was his forever rib. If he didn't know it or wasn't sure before tonight, he was positive right now.

Their eyes met and in the dark pools, Calvin saw life and love and never wanted to lose the feeling he got whenever he held he in his arms. Moving her flowing hair to the side, he placed soft kisses on her cheek before encircling her neck with them adding pressure the moment he heard a soft moan escape her lips. When he felt the movement of her swallowing hard, what was going to come next was undeniable. The night was meant to be about them and he never wanted to be any place other than in the arms making love to the woman he loved.

Turning off the music, Calvin took Ava's hand and headed to the bedroom. Stopping to briefly check that Camico was still sleeping and making sure they had the baby monitor, they walked hand in hand into the bedroom.

"I'm discovering the only thing that helps me tune out the bad in the world and focus on what's good and right is when you're in my arms. Come here, baby," he said pulling her close.

Pure lust surged through him when Ava came into his arms, wanting and desiring him as much as he did her. They were perfect together in every way.

Making swift work of their clothes, Calvin picked up a naked Ava, pulled back the thick down comforter and placed her on the bed, coming down onto it with her.

Together, they had become masters at foreplay, but tonight, he didn't make either of them wait. He needed to be inside of her.

"I know we love drawing out the pleasure, but that's not what I need tonight. I'm not a selfish lover though, so I'm putting it out here for you to tell me what you need. You know when we come together, it's important that I make it about you first," Calvin said in between hot, passionate kisses.

Already, his body was rock hard for her, especially that part that couldn't wait to get inside of her moistness.

"We never need a lot of pretense. All I need is you in whatever way we get there. I'm always on fire and ready for you," Ava said as she squirmed around under his powerful body loving the feel of him pressed into her.

Kissing Ava was always a necessity for him and tonight was no exception. The kiss went between being soft and pliant to hard and driven with a tugging need.

Reaching between them, Calvin tested her readiness for him and smiled when he encountered a pool of moisture at her womanly entrance. Using his fingers, he spread it around and watched the play of sensual emotion that crossed Ava's face.

"You get so wet for me," he whispered close to her ear.

Ava moaned and he knew she was in her zone, focusing on feeling.

"I love you," she said.

"I love you, too."

As the last word left his mouth, Calvin moved between her legs and positioned himself at her opening. Slipping inside of her, giving her a little bit of him at a time, trying to be tender, but sinfully driven to join them as one.

"I've been waiting for this big boy," she said, salaciously.

"It's all yours, baby," Calvin said before pushing himself as far inside of her welcoming body as he could go. Setting a pace that pleasured them both, he was driven on with a delicious sense of power as Ava's breaths quickened with uneven, muffled sounds as they moved together as one, letting the pleasure control them.

Pulling out, he surged in strong and he saw a troubled look on Ava's face. He stopped moving and captured a bewildered look on her face.

"Are you alright?"

"Am I hurting you?" he asked.

"No, you're not hurting me if that's what you're worried about. You feel amazing. All of my senses are acute to my pleasure every time you go in and out. I feel how hard you are and with every pass, I'm excited more and more. Don't stop," Ava declared and to prove her point, she lifted her hips from the bed, locked her legs around his back and showed him that she wanted all he had to give her.

"More?" he said.

"Yes, more," Ava murmured against his lips.

Before long, he had set a steady pace and when her womanly walls gripped him tight, he felt like a stallion running the race of his life. When Ava's cries of more filled his ears, he gave into the pleasure and gave her all of him as he surged, long and hard into her body. The wet sounds heard throughout the room from the slipperiness between them had him using all of the power he had regained in his legs to give her exactly what they both needed. Before long and without warning, Ava screamed his name as she pulled his lips down to hers. Calvin knew it was to muffle her screams as spasm after powerful spasm rocked into her causing her to flail about wildly under him.

Unable to hold off any longer, he wanted to join her and did, as shards of pleasure zapped him like a bolt of lightning sending him crashing with wave after wave as untamed sensations rocked him to his core.

As their bodies and breathing calmed and their movements slowed, Calvin kissed her as the impact of one of the most powerful orgasms of his life had his head spinning.

With his member still pulsing inside of her body, Ava refused to release him, loving the feel of him still long and hard inside of her. He felt hot and heavy and made just for her.

"You are so beautiful," Calvin said as plied her face with one kiss after another. "I will never tire of the look on your face as you come apart in my arms. I love you," he said.

"And I love you and in my arms, you will always find exactly what you need. I want to agree to always shut the world out when we're together and I don't mean only when we're together like this. I also mean when you, Camico and I are together. Let us be the strength you need when I know you're worried about protecting us."

"You are my world," Calvin said and leaned his head into the space between her head and her shoulders.

"As you are mine. We feel incredible together."

Calvin had to admit to himself something about making love this time was different. It was always good, but this time, it was better than any other time before and then something came to him. This time their lovemaking felt different because he forgot to use protection. He was so anxious to get inside of her with a need to overcame him, that he let the idea of protecting her slip his mind.

"I'm sorry, baby," he uttered.

"Sorry for what?" Ava asked, surprised that he would be apologizing.

"I forgot protection. In my haste to make love to you, my only thought was getting inside of you. I promise you, I'm good," he said.

"So am I."

"If you end up pregnant, you know I'll always be here. I'll always be yours, as long as you want me," he said.

"I want you forever and I'm on the pill. In our life together, we will have children when the time is right. Don't worry about anything," Ava said. "Sleep," she added.

Calvin moved to the side and pulled Ava snug into his body to spoon. With the baby monitor on the night stand and the woman he loved in his arms, Calvin didn't have a care in the world. He wouldn't live his life in fear of anything until it visited him head on. He was going to focus on the Ava and Camico – his heartbeats.

CHAPTER TWENTY-TWO

Calvin sat with Trey Blackwell in a restaurant about thirty minutes from his house. After the three weeks ago that he and Camico had spent at Ava's place, she had pretty much moved in with them. She still had her condo, but each day after she finished with her clients, she came home to his house with him and Camico. With the passage of time, they slid into a routine of hanging at his house or visiting with Cade and Callie and of course his niece, Colby. He had never seen Camico around his little cousin before, but Calvin could already see that he would make a great overprotective big brother.

A few times, he and Ava talked about their future together and they both agreed they wanted lots of children. He and his brothers didn't grow up with a large family and like him, Cade was looking forward to having a few more children as well.

He was thankful that for the past few weeks, he was able to relax and not worry. He and Mason had been in touch and after he approached this Admiral about his connection to Valencio, nothing surfaced that bridged a gap between him and Valencio. There had been no other word on the horizon about signs of Valencio in South America. They agreed he was either hiding out or working on new illegal activities, giving up on the fact that his grandson was out there somewhere, but he didn't know where.

Earlier in the day, Trey had called to say he had touched down in Texas and was picking up a truck that was more like an armored money truck. Inside of it, he had brought over with him on the private plane he flew in on, a wealth of various weaponry and other electronic surveillance devices and equipment. They were going to have their talk about going into business together and Calvin's decision was made. He'd had his taste of domestic life with Camico and Ava and he wasn't going to turn back. He needed to be a parent who was present.

After Ava came in from work, he told her about his meeting with Trey and wanted her and Camico to go to Cade's house and he would pick them up when he returned. Ava insisted she and Camico would be fine until he returned. The alarm could be set and she was going to feed Camico his dinner, get him a bath and then take a hot bath herself to wait for him in their favorite place – the bed.

He had reservations about leaving them, but he

had made her a promise that he would look to their future together and not looking to the past. It had been a lot of months since he first returned to the United States injured and all had been quiet. He promised her he would only be gone for a little while and that he'd be less than an hour away. He reminded her about the panic rooms throughout the house, where the weapons were and how to operate the security system. They had spent many nights in the house with nothing happening, so there was no need to worry.

Kissing Ava and Camico, he exited the house through the garage, got in his truck and left to meet Trey.

Thirty minutes later, he pulled up to the restaurant and as they reminisced about old times, they finally got into the reason for the meeting.

"Have you made a decision about going back in?" Trey asked.

Calvin without hesitation knew he was ready to answer, but knowing how Trey felt about being a navy SEAL, he didn't want to look like he was turning his back on his commitment to his country. He would still give his life for his country at any time, but he also had a commitment to his son. He needed to be around for Camico and being away for months at a time is not the kind of father he wanted to be. Being injured taught him a lot; family was everything. He could protect them more by being with them

234

"I'm not going back. There are a lot of reasons and most involve being there for my son who has already lost his mother. I know it will be weeks before I'm fully functional again in order to get an exam and be cleared to return to regular duty. I've come a long way much quicker than they thought, but as vigorous as assignments for SEALs are, who knows how long it would be before I was one hundred percent. I've learned a lot over the past few months and that is how much my family means to me and how much I've missed out on. My little brother is about to graduate college and go on to graduate school. I have a new niece and sister-in-law and I can't leave Ava out."

"That's getting pretty serious, huh?"

Calvin smiled. Just the thought of knowing that once he and Trey parted ways tonight, he was rushing to get back to his house where Ava would no doubt be waiting for him in something slinky and sexy – just the way he liked.

"It is. I'm in love with her and the way she is with my son, I think he prefers her over me most days, but I'm okay with that. I would prefer her, too," he joked.

"Yeah, she and Kensi are very close – more like sisters from where they met working in the hospital together. After that mess of rescuing her sister and brother almost a year ago, I got a chance to know more about Ava and she is an incredible woman. When I recommended her for your rehabilitation, I had a feeling things would get tricky."

"Tricky is an understatement. Ava is beautiful and any man would be crazy to not see that."

"How are things on the Valencio front? Any word on his location?" Trey asked.

"That's the crazy thing. So far, nothing and no sightings. Something tells me I should be more aware. Mason has been looking into one lead after another and he's planning to take a team back to South America in about a week. He's been given the green light to go back in and look for Valencio. At one time, he thought he had a lead and a leak in our country high up in the ranks that was assisting Valencio, but that didn't pan out. Doesn't mean it wasn't true. You know Admiral Munson?"

"Yeah, I do. You think it's him?" Trey asked.

"Mason was able to get some contacts to look into the Admiral's finances and assets and he's living way beyond his means. Behind the scenes, that's being investigated. We'll see what comes out of that."

"Everything secure at the house?"

"Yes, your guys did an amazing job on the house. That place is like Fort Knox on the inside, but I need to work on perimeter security. There is always a way in and I didn't want the house to look like a prison. It needs to feel like home for my family. Ava is there now with Camico waiting for me to get home after you head off to the airport to get home to your wife. Did you say Kensi was pregnant?"

"Yes, I did and we are over the top with excitement. We have one daughter, Kylie, the baby she was pregnant with when her husband Kyle died. That baby knows no other father, but me and this will be my first. We just found out it's a boy and we both wanted a boy."

"Congratulations! I know the feeling of excitement you're talking about. When I found out about Camico, from that point on, nothing mattered but him and his mother. The worse day of my life was when she died as a result of my falling in love with her. For a long time, I carried that blame because if I hadn't come into her life, her life wouldn't have been at risk. I knew the dangerous man her father was and if he could have her mother killed to protect himself, he wouldn't hesitate to have Sofia killed if she got in the way."

"Cal, you know you can't think that way. From what you tell me about her, Sofia loved you and she wouldn't want that. She would want you to make sure Camico is safe from her father."

"You're doing that. You said there was no sign of Valencio anywhere in South America? He's hiding someplace," Trey said.

"As long as it's not her, I'm good."

Calvin was about to say something else when his cell phone rang and Mason's name popped up. He was about to speak when Mason spoke up first.

"Cal, where are you man!" Mason shouted.

Hearing the worried and hurried tone in

Mason's voice, Calvin stood so fast, the bar stool turned over behind him. He went to reach for it when Trey got to it first.

"I'm out with Trey. What's going on? You sound like you're running," he said.

"That's exactly what I'm doing and I'm heading your way. I'm thirty minutes away, but I'll make it there in fifteen. We have a problem. Are you and Trey close to your house and if not, are Ava and Camico there alone?"

Calvin pulse quickened when Mason asked about his son.

"No, I'm about thirty or so minutes from my house and Camico is there with Ava. What's going on?" Calvin said, now terrified that something was wrong.

"This is bad, Cal. Valencio is in the states and he's been here for over a month – more like six weeks and he knows who you are. I think he's coming for you tonight. I took some guys with me to the property way up in the Colorado mountains where he's been staying at a condo owned Admiral Munson. Apparently, he's been feeding information about you to the Valencio. I was able to convince some top officials of his involvement. We went to talk to him and he knew things were turning bad for him. That's when he told us everything including the fact that two weeks ago, he gave you up to Valencio and he has men who are coming for you and they're doing it tonight, as we speak. We were able to take down one of Valencio's men who was at the house in Colorado with Munson and he said that they've been watching you for a few days. They're already in Texas and someplace close to your house. Seems like Munson smuggled Valencio into the country undetected and he's been hiding out at that house in Colorado. I don't know if he's with his men or not, but he's got a crew of six heading your way."

Calvin threw some money on the counter to cover their meal and hurried to make his way back home with Trey following close behind.

"What do you know? Does he know where I live exactly? Does he know about my family?" Calvin asked as they hustled.

"Yeah, Cal. He knows and by now, he knows you're not at the house. I saw some photos that were sent to Valencio's guy that we took out and there were lots of pictures of you, Camico and Ava. None of anyone else in your family. Valencio wants Camico alive and you dead. We need to get there," Mason screamed.

"I'm already on my way and I have Trey with me."

"I'm on my way buddy and I have eight guys with me. You have any gear that's not at the house?" Mason asked.

Calvin jumped in the passenger seat of Trey's truck and barely had the door closed before Trey barreled out of there.

"My gear is all at the house and in my truck," he said. "I gathered what was in my truck and I'm in Trey's truck with him."

"I've got plenty of gear – more than you'll ever need. We're locked, loaded and ready," Trey said, already weaving in and out of traffic.

"I'm on my way," Mason said and hung up.

Calvin disconnected the call and immediately dialed the house phone. He tapped his foot waiting for Ava to answer and after a few rings, the voice mail system kicked in. He hung up and this time dialed her cell phone, praying she would answer.

CHAPTER TWENTY-THREE

Ava grabbed the baby monitor and after covering up Camico, she walked into the master bedroom and looked around at the tons of toys sprawled out across the floor. Seeing them brought a huge smile to her face.

After her last client for the day, she could hardly wait to run home, check on her condo and then head over to Calvin's house to enjoy a relaxing evening with them. For several weeks now, after they'd spent the night at her place and Camico woke in the morning happy to see her, they have been spending practically every night together.

She was glad they were able to relax more after weeks of Calvin being worried about threats. A lot of time had passed and now they were thinking they could push the worrying to the back burner. They settled into a routine like any other family would and now that Calvin was back to his normal routine and up to running over five miles a day, he felt strong enough to now start making moves towards what he wanted to do career wise. They had talked a few times where he sounded resolved to being close to home, but she could still see the struggle and the pull to return to his military life.

Calvin had once told her that he couldn't remember a time in his life when he didn't want to be a soldier and once he began training as a SEAL, he knew it's what he was meant to be – in a position to keep Americans safe. Now, he was faced with the option to still do that, but on a more local setting. Working with other former SEALs he would run operations of a protective, security nation right out of Texas. He would still have to go on assignments, some even abroad, but never would he be gone for months at a time again.

Tonight, after she arrived, Calvin had been preparing to meet with Trey who had arrived in town for a meeting and to do some site scouting for a location for the office complex they would need. He had been preparing Camico for a night with Callie and she wondered why. When she asked him, he said he didn't want to put the burden on her to look after Camico. When she asked if he didn't trust her with his son, he quickly explained it was nothing like that. They were able to iron out the fact that as a couple, he and Camico were a packaged deal and she loved being a part of the two of them. She would do anything for him and Camico and if she was going to be at the house waiting for him to return, he shouldn't uproot Camico – they would be fine at home together.

Strolling around the bedroom after Camico's bath and a little more play time, she gathered up one toy after the other. Next up would be a hot shower before changing into something slinky and sexy for Calvin's return. When she stopped at home earlier, she picked up a sexy little one-piece silver and black lingerie set and couldn't wait for Calvin to see her in it. Their intimate life never had a dull moment and she loved surprising him with the unexpected.

With the house securely locked up and Camico sound asleep, she grabbed the baby monitor and headed into the shower.

~~

"I can't reach her. Something's wrong," Calvin said as Trey sped through traffic.

"I'm sure she's fine and may have her phone on vibrate. Has she ever answered your house phone before? If not, that may be why she didn't answer that assuming if you called, you would call her cell phone. We'll be there any minute, so don't worry."

"That's my woman and my son. I should be worried and I never should have let my guard down. The look I saw in Valencio's eyes that day at his house told me he would never give up on getting Camico back. I should have known."

"You did know, which is why you made your house as secure as you did."

"Right, but that's only if someone gets inside. I was planning on securing the outside grounds and even had a contractor lined up for next week. What if someone has already gotten inside of the house without Ava knowing it. Anything could be happening to them right now!" Calvin shouted.

"Who can you call that's close by to help?" Trey asked.

"I could call Callie's father, but his property is further away than we are and his men wouldn't get there until after us."

"Call him anyway. We need someone with eyes on that house," Trey said.

Calvin began dialing.

~~

"Valencio, we're here. We've been watching the house for a few hours from a distance and whoever this guy is, he must be loaded. American's sure live large," one of Valencio's men said.

Valencio smiled. His men are getting close to getting him what he wanted.

"I don't care what his house looks like. Do not hurt even one hair on my grandson's head. His safety is your most important priority," he said.

Valencio paced the small, out of the way motel room as he waited to hear that his men had Camico and were heading back to him. As he looked around the dirty, centuries old room with stained walls, floors and blankets, he kept his cool and every few minutes, peered out of the curtain to be sure he saw no movement. He was still taking a risk of being found out and he couldn't have that happening.

Being in Texas was risky without being able to connect with Admiral Munson who had been his eyes and ears for the past few months.

"We understand, sir. As we mentioned, only the woman and your grandson appear to be at the house. We watched the soldier leave a few hours ago and you told us to focus on getting your grandson and to wait for him to return to deal with him."

"That's right. I need to get Camico out of their first and then this soldier needs to be dealt with. What are you seeing?" he asked.

"We can't see anything. Even though we can see lights on inside, he must have some special kind of windows that prevent us from seeing anything clearly happening on the inside.

"What about movement outside?" he asked.

"Nothing from what we can see. A woman showed up a few hours ago and right after, your soldier left out. We're waiting for your orders to go in. We're not sure about the security he has in place, though we're sure there is something. With him not being here, we shouldn't much of a fight from some woman. What do you want us to do with her?"

"I don't care what you do with her. Get my grandson and get back here. I haven't heard from my contact yet, but I'm trusting he still has our transportation back to South America ready at a moment's notice."

"Should we move now?"

"Yes, make your move now and keep me posted. The minute you have my grandson, I want to know and then leave a few men around to deal with that soldier. I want him to remember what he did to me," Valencio said and hung up. Now, he had to play the waiting game.

~~

Coming out of the shower, Ava was mad at herself for forgetting one rule from Calvin that he stressed time and again when she was at the house without him. He told her to always remember to have the satellite phone within her reach. He'd purchased one specifically to leave at the house and he never left the house without his. His brother had given one to each of his brothers because they were often in different parts of the country at any given time and he wanted to be able to reach them always.

She'd left it in the bedroom when she went into the bathroom to shower and change for bed. She remembered to take Camico's baby monitor to listen out for him, but she forgot the phone. If Calvin had been trying to reach her, he would call her cell phone, so she didn't feel too bad about forgetting it.

Leaving the bathroom, she saw the phone sitting on the dresser next to her cell phone and was about to grab it to put it on the nightstand right next to the bed when the lights in the room flickered, once, twice and then three times. Startled, she didn't move. Having her own brief military background, she quickly became aware of every immediate sound or visual change. As her heart rate sped up, she stood still and waited to see if anything else out of the ordinary would happen. She felt secure that she and Camico were safe, something Cal had taken great care to put in place.

He'd told her about the panic room and what it meant in case of any emergency if he was home or not. Any sign of danger, she was to grab Camico and head for that room. There was an entrance on both levels of the house hidden behind panels that looked like ordinary walls. Her instincts told her to think over everything she needed to know, just in case.

Hearing nothing else, she still felt uneasy. Instead of slipping on the sexy nightie she'd bought to wear for Calvin, she hurried into the closet and grabbed a black sweat suit she kept at his house and slipped her feet inside of a pair of her sneakers that had been close to the door. She pulled her hair into a ponytail while shutting off the lights in the room, sending it into extreme darkness. Walking over to the window, she looked out over the dark night sky and looked around the grounds of the house to see if there was any movement. Seeing none, she backed away and remembered to grab the satellite phone. She had an uneasy feeling even though the lights didn't go completely out.

As she thought about Camico and the need to

check on him, she grabbed both phones and Camico's monitor and rushed to his room while still listening for any unusual sounds. Seeing Camico still asleep, she breathed a sigh of relief which lasted only a second because the satellite phone rang. Something was wrong and perhaps the lights flickering was something to worry about.

"Calvin? What's going on?" she said.

"Ava, are you and Camico okay?" he said.

Her nerves rattled hearing the worry in Calvin's voice. He was trying his best to remain calm, but it wasn't working.

"We're fine. I put him to bed about an hour ago and I just got out of the shower. The lights in the house blinked. Is something going on?" she asked, trying to remain calm.

"Listen to me very carefully. Trey and I are about minute from the house. I think there are men at the house who are going to try and get inside to get Camico. Mason and a team are making their way to the house right now on foot. I can already see the house. Have you heard any sounds inside of the house? Are the alarm lights still on in each room? Where are you?" he asked.

"I'm in Camico's room. I sensed something strange when the lights flickered. I grabbed the phones and came right to his room to check on him. I was about to call you."

"I've been calling your cell phone and the house phone and you didn't answer either which is why I called the satellite."

"I'm sorry about that. I was in the shower."

"Don't worry about it, baby. I hear your voice and I'm good knowing you're good. Mason called while I was out with Trey and had information that Valencio is in the states and headed to the house. Looks like he's been here for a while and no one knew other than an Admiral who has been helping him. He may have had men watching us for a while and that means they know I'm not there with you."

Ava's worry changed to terrified and her instinct to protect Camico was all that she was concerned about.

"Did you call the police? What should I do?" she asked, frightened as she stood in the middle of Camico's room with him over her shoulder after picking him up. Whatever was next, it wouldn't involve them staying in the bedroom. While Calvin talked she went into action. She walked over to Camico's closet and grabbed the ready-prepared getaway bag Calvin always kept packed in case of an emergency. She threw it over her shoulder and walked to the window, careful to stay on the side of it, allowing her to peer out. With her naked eye, she couldn't see anything even with the bright, powerful lights that surrounded the property.

"I can't call the police. There would be too much to explain and not enough time to do it knowing you and Camico could be in danger. All I can remember is what happened to Sofia and I can't have anything happen to you and my son. Now, listen baby, you and I have gone over the 'in case of emergency' plan and you know what to do. I don't know if anyone is coming or if so, how much time you have, so listen to me closely."

Ava focused on his words and nothing else just as the lights around the property went dark along with the lights in the house. Though the lights were already out in Camico's room because he was asleep, she could see through the bedroom door that the lights across the hall were dark and she no longer heard the television. She held Camico closer.

"Calvin, the lights just went completely out, even the ones outside. I don't think there is any power to the house," she said frightened and happy Camico was asleep. She wouldn't want to scare him.

"Baby, don't wait for anything else. You know where to go. Get into the panic room using the entrance in Camico's room. You remember the code? That's the only safe place in the house for you and the baby, so get there now. I'm on my way to you in a few seconds. We pulled up to a secluded spot. Mason and his men are here, too. I don't care what happens, until I open that door, don't you move."

"You don't want me to go through the tunnel to the truck at the end and drive away from here?" she asked.

"No, because I don't know if information on that entrance may have been compromised. Those doors are military grade steel and no one can get in without the code and the only people who have it are you, me and my brothers. Are you heading in? Do it now!" he screamed.

"Okay," Ava said hearing the shakiness in her own voice.

"Now, baby. No hesitation. Take the phone with you. It's the only one that will work behind the walls of the panic room."

Ava didn't wait and didn't take time to think about what could be happening around or in the house. She moved Camico's crib and pushed on the base of the wall until she heard a click. Instantly a panel on the wall opened and she slipped inside with Camico in her arms. As soon as she was on the other side, the crib automatically moved back into place and the panel on the wall went back into place. Anyone entering the room would see a wall that looked like a jungle and unless they were looking for a panel to a secret room, they wouldn't see it with all of the creative artwork.

Now that she was behind the wall, she walked a few steps and came up to a large steel door that looked like a bank vault.

"I'm at the panic room door about to put the code in," she said. Nervously, she typed in the seven numbers and the pressure door opened. She stepped back to allow the door to fully open and listening for any noise she may be able to hear in the house, she halted a few seconds. "I think I hear something," she said.

"Ava, don't stop. You should be inside already. Get in and seal the door back," he said. He was rushing to them, but first needed to know they were safely inside. He had no doubt once they were inside, he wouldn't have to worry about them. No one was getting in there. Even if the house was leveled, the secure areas behind the walls of his house would still be standing. There are people, he knew, who would think it was excessive, but with what he knew being a navy SEAL, it was his way of being prepared for all kinds of disasters and not just the kind on two feet that he knew were already at his house knowing he wasn't there.

"Okay, I'm inside and the big steel door just closed back behind us."

As soon as she said that, lights inside along the floor and ceiling illuminated the space and she could see her way around.

Her eyes widened in amazement at what she saw. There were huge television screens that illuminated the outside of the house all around it. There were also monitors in every room of the house. There were large cabinets are large military style bins lined along the wall. The size of the room is what amazed her the most. She couldn't figure out how the size was masked by the even larger bedrooms inside the house. There were high-tech computers all around her and even though she remembered the lights outside and inside had gone out, she could see everything as if the lights were still on.

When she turned around, she spotted a crib that Calvin had placed in the room. He had planned ahead for any kind of emergency. She placed Camico in the crib and made sure he wasn't startled awake.

"Okay, I need you to look at any of the screens and tell me what you see. They should show all the rooms inside of the house and the exterior. If you push the white button underneath the largest screen, the hidden cameras outside of the house will tell you if anyone is on the grounds. What do you see?" he asked.

Ava found the button, pushed it and in an instant, she could see six shadowy figures, all with large guns. Three were in the front of the house, panning out and the others were in the back of the house, covering every entrance they could see.

"I see six figures. Are you here yet? Are any of those you?" she asked.

"No, baby, that's not me. We're parked and now that I know you're safe, we're working out a plan. Remember, they can't get to you and Camico as long as you stay put. Even if they find the panic rooms, they can't get in. Even in Camico cries, those rooms are all soundproof. There is a crib for him in the room if you want to lay him back down."

"I did that. I'm sitting in front of one of the screens," she said.

"Good. You are completely safe as long as you don't open any of the steel doors that lead to the room. Once I've taken care of this threat, I will open them from my side. If anything happens to me and I'm not saying it will, but just in case, you are not to open any door. If I'm not in that room before daybreak, you call Cade and when it's safe to come out, he'll come and get you."

"Calvin," Ava cried.

"I know, baby. Don't cry. Everything is going to be okay. I'm not going to let anything happen to you and my baby boy."

"What about you?" she said, crying, but trying to stifle them to not wake Camico.

"Trust me, I don't want to leave you and Camico, but I will die protecting you if I have to. Just don't open the door and after I hang up, turn off the cameras to the house. I don't want you to see anything that happens. Promise me you will turn them off," he said.

"I promise."

"Good. I will call you when this is done. Watch out for Camico. There are comfortable places in there for you to wait this out and plenty of food, water and formula for him if he wakes up. I love you, Ava. I love you, baby!" Calvin said.

"I love you, too," Ava said.

"Hang up, baby."

Ava turned the satellite phone off and like she promised him, she turned off the screens on the monitors and walked further into the maze until she came to a small room with the sofas and beds. She pulled Camico's crib along with her.

In the room and able to think a little clearer, she covered Camico and looked around. Remembering a conversation she and Calvin had a few weeks back about the panic rooms, she remembered where the weapons were.

Seeing a panel on the wall, she entered the code Calvin had given her for that safe, she opened it and withdrew two weapons. She placed one inside of her duffle along with extra bullets and the other she kept in her hand. She didn't think she'd have a need for it, but she would kill anything that moved in that space that wasn't her or Camico. Sitting on the floor next to Camico's crib, she waited.

CHAPTER TWENTY-FOUR

Calvin exhaled a sigh of relief knowing Ava and Camico were safe. The minute that Trey stopped the truck, he was out of it and heading around to the back to get his hands on the weaponry in the back. He was thankful for the coincidence of Trey bringing weapons and gear to showcase at a local gun show and now they were about to put them to good use.

"All good at your house?" Trey asked.

"Thanks to you and your men, yes. They're secure as long as those doors hold up," he said as he worked.

"Trust me, they'll hold. Grab a headset and you'll find all black attire in the box in the back," Trey said.

Calvin grabbed the weapons he knew he would need.

"I need to get to the house!" he shouted louder than he wanted to. There was no way anyone would know about this spot a half a mile from his house.

As soon as he spoke, Calvin felt a hand on his shoulder.

"Bro, we're here and we got this. Those guys are going to wish they had never heard about you or Camico. If Valencio isn't with them, we'll deal with him next. I already have a plan in place and it won't require any outside help. You trust me?" Mason said.

"With my life."

"Good, then lets go get your woman and your son." Mason turned to the men he brought with him. "Okay, I gave you all the layout of the house and from what we know, they're on the property, but not in the house, yet. I'm sure that'll change within minutes so let's go. No one survives besides Ava and Camico. They'll never get the chance to come back again," he added.

"You think Valencio is with them?" Calvin asked.

"Not on your life. He sent his goons, but I hear he doesn't have the balls to do any of his own dirty work," Trey responded.

Trey dressed and pulled one weapon after the other and found a place on him to load everything up.

"I'm going to kill him. You know that, right?" Calvin said and meant every word.

"I hear you, but right now, let's deal with what's in front of us and come back around to deal with Valencio Ramirez. If my assessment is true and he's not here, we won't get the support from the military to go back into South America to take him out. We're going to have to do this just like Mason said. For now, focus and let's do this."

After making sure Cal was ready, Trey locked the truck and they headed off through the woods with Mason and his men spreading out.

"Mason? Can are you there?" Cal asked speaking into his headset as they ran, staying close to the ground.

"I'm here partner. What's up?"

"I told Ava to stay in the panic room, but if for any reason, she comes out..."

"I hear ya. Nothing is going to happen to her and Camico. Trust me on that," Mason acknowledged as they moved onto his property.

Staying hunched down, Calvin could see the house and how dark Ava said it was. He could also see movement and before moving forward, he put in a quick call to Cade. He spoke up before Cade could get a word in.

"Problems at my house. Make sure the family stays clear of it," he said hurriedly.

"What's going on Cal and where is Camico?" Cade asked.

"He's safe. Are you here in Texas?" he asked.

"Yes. I'm here at Callie's parents' house about to head home."

"Don't move and let Callie's father know to get his men along with yours on point to protect all of you. The safest place is definitely on his property and I'll fill you in soon. I'm safe and so is Camico, so don't worry. Where's Cam?" he asked.

"He's in Los Angeles doing an interview for an internship at a major television network."

"Okay, he's fine, but just to be sure, do you have men you can contact to keep an eye on him? It's Valencio. He's here in the states and he's coming for me. If he knows who I am, he may know about you and Cam, too."

"I'm on it, bro. Anyone with you to watch your six?" Cade asked making reference to men having his back.

Calvin laughed.

"Yeah, I have a band of brothers and they are about business. I'll get with you as soon as I can. Keep the family safe," Calvin said and hung up.

"Let's move," he said in his headset and he watched as everyone moved into place.

~~

Ava had been sitting on the floor beside Camico's crib for what seemed like an eternity, but was probably more like a few hours. Thankfully, Camico had played so hard before bed that she was sure he would sleep through the night. Whatever was happening on the other side of the wall, she couldn't hear and even though she was tempted to go back and cut the monitors back on so that she could see, she'd made a promise.

The waiting was eating away at her, but her main priority was keeping Camico safe and Calvin was counting on her. During the past few hours that she'd been in this space, she took a little time to explore, not going too far from Camico. What she encountered was out of this world. There was no doubt that in any kind of emergency situation, anyone in this space could survive for a long time. She even saw medical equipment and it looked as if Calvin replaced it often making sure nothing was expired. There was extra clothing, bedding and every household need imaginable. She wondered if others lived like this or was it just soldiers like Calvin who saw destruction everyday and knew what to prepare for. She was thankful for a man like him.

For years, she feared falling in love with anyone in case her identity ended up being compromised, putting someone else in danger if she were found. She never expected to find herself in danger again, but this time, she found herself responsible for someone other than herself. Knowing that Calvin was outside protecting her put her at ease. She had no doubt he was doing everything in his power to alleviate the threat while she did her part inside the room. She would wait as long as Calvin asked her to and prayed silently that she wouldn't have to call for help because he would open the door.

Hearing Camico whimper, she stood to check on him just as she heard a sound. Not sure what it was, she moved back toward the room with the monitors and listened. Sure enough, she could hear what sounded like a code being entered into the keypad. She moved about nervously, hoping it was Calvin, but just in case it wasn't, she raised her weapon and aimed it right at the door. If it was someone coming for Camico who shouldn't be, she wasn't going to make it easy for them.

Within seconds as she braced herself, the door moved slightly.

"Ava? It's me," Calvin said.

Ava expelled the breath she was holding and as soon as she saw his face peer around the side, she ran into his arms and released the cry she'd been holding in.

"You're okay!" she shouted and kissed as much of his face as she could find.

"I'm fine, baby. I told you I would be."

"Camico is sleeping in the other room. Are you sure you're alright?" she asked again, now looking him over.

"I'm fine."

Ava looked up as Trey entered the room behind him.

"You're good?" Trey said looking around without lowering his weapon yet.

"Yes. No one tried to get in and I've been in the other room sitting on the floor next to Camico's crib the whole time," she said.

"Holding that thing?" Calvin said smiling.

"No one was getting Camico from me," she declared.

"Trust me, they never will. You, me and Camico are a team – we're family and no one will ever break that up. I love you, baby," Calvin said and kissed her like he meant it.

When he pulled back she looked in his eyes and knew that their love was a forever kind of love.

"What happened out there?" she asked.

Calvin looked from her to Trey and then back to her.

"Let's just say there's no longer a threat on my property and soon, there won't be a threat at all. Right now, there are officers in the house and around the grounds handling things and for now, I'm going to stay right here with you and Camico until I get the all clear from Trey and Mason. They'll take care of what's going on out there and for now, I'm going to take care of the two of you in here."

"Are you sure everything is over? Valencio?" she asked.

"He wasn't with them. We just got a call that the place where he was, he's no longer there. There's no doubt, he's gone back into hiding, but I will find him and he and I are going to have this out once and for all. He's never getting my son and I'm going to see to it that he's not around anymore to even think about it. Right now, let's go inside and let the authorities handle everything."

"What about the rest of your family?" she asked.

"They're fine. I was able to reach Cade and he

took care of making sure everyone was safe including Cam who's in California. Everyone is fine. What about you? I know it must have been hell no knowing what was going on."

"It was, but I knew you would take care of it. I know you would give your life for that little guy and you wouldn't let anyone get to him."

"I would give my life for you, too. You and Camico are why my heart beats. I wouldn't be able to live if anything happened to either one of you. I have to deal with Valencio now and that means I may have to go away for a little bit. I have to track him down once and for all or this will never end."

"Where are you going?" she asked.

"I'm going wherever he is," Calvin said picking Camico up from the crib and cradling him while he slept.

"He's not going to stop, is he?"

"I don't think he ever will which is why I have to do something. I let my guard down this time because I didn't think we would be vulnerable. I never thought someone in my own country who is suppose to be loyal to it would be caught betraying the very country he swore to protect. That man put my entire family at risk for money. That's unforgiveable and now, Valencio is again running free and doing so in this country. I don't doubt he will find a way to get out and wherever he goes, I will be there."

Calvin reached down and brought Ava's face

close to his. Seeing her face again was what kept him focused as he fought Valencio's men.

Once they made it to the house, he found that the men had breached an entrance to his house through the garage, but before they could get off of the first floor, they went from firing shot after shot at each other to some hand to hand fighting. When the men wouldn't stop their pursuit, he, Trey, Mason and the crew had no choice, but to put them all down. One man who didn't want to die for Valencio surrendered and told them everything, including where Valencio was hiding and waiting for them. He also said that they had warned Valencio that they encountered men at the house during the gunfight and he was sure Valencio took that opportunity to run and hide and most likely try to flee back to his own country where he had others who would protect him.

"I would say I'm not worried, but I am and I will be until you return."

"Believe me, I want to return to you and Camico as much as you do and that's my plan. I have an idea of how I can get to Valencio and I won't have to personally lay a hand on him. I don't need to do that for my own satisfaction. My only concern is making sure he won't come back into our lives again. Thank you for protecting my son," he said.

Calvin would share more, but he wouldn't. He didn't want her to know that he was going to use the one man from Valencio's squad to get information on how to get close to Valencio. He hoped that in no time at all, his waiting around for Valencio's vengeance to show up would be over.

"I would do it again and again."

"When I return, I want to talk about our lives becoming one with you, me and Camico. I need to get this weight of Valencio Ramirez off of me before I can move on and moving on is my priority."

Ava smiled. Everything Calvin said sounded like music to her ears. Her life was about her favorite two people, father and son.

CHAPTER TWENTY-FIVE

Calvin made his way through the underground passage knowing there wasn't a threat against him inside. Valencio thought he was safe being back in his own country, but thanks to a plan that he and Mason worked out, he felt as safe as he does when he's at home.

Using the instructions from one of Valencio's men, he walked through the maze and came upon a large black door that was opened. He was able to peer around the side of it and find Valencio sitting behind a large marble-topped desk smoking a cigar. He raised his weapon and moved inside. The moment Valencio saw him, he attempted to reach for what Calvin assumed was a weapon and warned him.

"I wouldn't do that," he said.

Calvin watched as a variety of emotions showed on Valencio's face, none the least being how he was able to get this close without encountering his men who stood guard around the clock.

"So, you're here to kill me all by yourself? Where is your military?" Valencio asked.

"I don't need my military. You made this personal the minute you sent men to my home to try and kidnap my son. What you should be asking is where are your men? Aren't you wondering how I was able to not only find you, but do so through all of those men you have guarding this fortress?"

Calvin knew he had a smug look on his own face and hoped it pissed Valencio off. He was feeling quite smug and was happy that things would soon be over.

"I don't care about any men. I assume they're dead because that's the only way you could have gotten in here. As far as kidnapping my grandson - I didn't have to kidnap what is already mine. He is my flesh and blood. You turned my daughter against me and you killed my son."

"He was yours and only by blood. My son belonged to your daughter and me and she never wanted you anywhere near him. I promised her that and I plan to keep that promise. I didn't turn Sofia away from you. You did that the minute you had her mother killed for wanting to get away from you. Sofia had been trying to get away from you for a while and I was her ticket out and you ended that. As for your son, he had that bullet coming for him. The things he'd done could only be responded to by a bullet, same as you. You are a vile man, Valencio and I came all this way to tell you that," Calvin said with disdain in his voice.

"If you think you'll get out of Colombia alive after killing me, you are mistaken."

Calvin laughed while keeping his weapon trained on Valencio's head. He would love to pull the trigger and end the back and forth, but what was in store for Valencio was much worse. His only regret was not being around when it happened.

"Really? You still feel that way? I was able to get this close to you and yet I don't hear anyone rushing to your rescue. Where are your men? Oh, that's right, they are gone and probably already spending your millions which they now have access to. Your men aren't loyal to you – they were loyal to your money and now that they see they can have one without the other, they chose money. There is no one around but you and me. Here we are, two men who hate each other and only one of us will survive this meet and greet," Calvin said.

The satisfaction he felt finally able to give Valencio a piece of his mind was only matched by the fact that in a few days, he'd be back home with his son and Ava without any threat against them again.

"You think it's going to be you who's going to survive? Do you know who I am? Do you know the kind of power I wield every day? I have men on payroll in your military and pretty high up I must say for a man like me who never even finished school. You think killing me will be the end? My men will never stop coming for you!" Valencio shouted and stood.

Calvin laughed at his arrogance. Even now with a high-powered weapon aimed at his head not knowing if he would pull the trigger or not, he was still defiant as if he was in control.

"You are finished Valencio and you're the only one who doesn't know that. I think I hear footsteps now," Calvin said moving backwards toward the door.

"That's probably my men you hear. You won't get out alive," Valencio said.

Calvin laughed again.

"Not only will I get out of here alive, I'm going to go back to my country and enjoy raising the son that Sofia and I made together. He will know everything about her and nothing about you. He will live the life she always wanted to live, far away from you and soon, you will be a distant memory for me, too. I would say it's been nice finally meeting you, but it hasn't been. It will be nice knowing you won't be around to wreak havoc on anyone else's life. I know that there will be men who will come up after you're dead and try to take your place, but there will always be forces that will combat any of their activity. People are tired of living the way they do because you allow them to. They want freedom from you and your tyranny and I'm going to help them out with that. You can go ahead and have a seat because you're not going anywhere. You should have stuck with your pitiful life here and never come after me and my son. In a few minutes, you will see why," Calvin said.

Before Valencio could act, he stepped out of the room and bolted it shut from the other side. There were no other exits from the room. The minute he was sure Valencio wouldn't be able to leave the room, he rushed out and signaled to his men he was free. Seconds after he was several feet away, he nodded and while still running, the entire building imploded and with the amount of explosives used to wire the place, there would be no way Valencio would have been able to survive. Valencio's men had told him exactly where and how to wire the place.

When he was some distance away, he grabbed his binoculars and looked back at what he saw. He was glad to see that nothing survived that blast. All he saw was fire, smoke and dust. There was no way to tell a building once stood in that spot.

"Cal? Where are you?"

Hearing Mason's voice, he grabbed his headset and reconnected it.

"I'm here and I'm good. We'll meet at the rendezvous spot," he said and turned and walked away. "I need to make one stop and I'll be at the chopper. Don't leave without me," Calvin said.

"We're not going anywhere without you," Mason said.

Jumping in the jeep that he'd hidden, another

man from his team joined him and hopped into the driver's seat.

"You want me to drive you there now?" he asked.

Calvin knew he had to make this one stop because he wasn't planning on coming back to Colombia ever again. He needed to be sure his plans were being carried out. His commanding officer had called in some pretty big favors to make this happen for him.

As they drove, he thought about Sofia and the freedom he knew she was now experiencing in death that she was never allowed to experience in life. He smiled at how much Camico looked like her, especially his eyes. They were the first thing about Sofia that he noticed when he saw her and he would now see those eyes in their son for the rest of his life.

They had driven about ten miles when they came upon the spot where Sofia had been buried along with her mother. He could see that men were furiously working to unearth her remains so that they could be prepared for transport to the United States where he had already secured a plot for her remains. He wanted Camico to always know where his mother was buried and that he would be able to visit her final resting place anytime he wanted.

As Sofia's coffin was loaded onto the back of a truck to be driven to a place where she'd be placed in the coffin he'd brought over with him, he said a silent prayer and hoped that she was smiling down knowing that even if she could not have gotten out of Colombia to live out her life in America, her remains would.

He waved at the men as the waved at him letting him know that his wishes had been carried out. He would be flying back in the carrier that would fly Sofia to the United States. He'd secured a funeral home already that would meet the flight and immediately give Sofia the proper burial she deserved.

~~

Ava paced around the house hoping she wouldn't disturb anyone else, but she was worried about Calvin. She hadn't heard from him since the moment he flew out to Colombia almost two weeks ago.

After the gunfight and destruction at his house as a result of it, Calvin had men who would be working on repairs and installing private fencing around the entire property. He asked her to stay with Cade and Callie on Callie's father's ranch where he knew she and Camico would be around people who cared about them and would look after them while he was gone.

Calvin told her he had to finish what he started. Valencio got away from him the first time, but not this time. Now, he and Mason had gathered a team who would be going in after Valencio and dealing with him once and for all.

She and Camico found comfort with Cade and

Callie and the time their helped her develop a strong bond with Callie. She'd also learned a lot more about Calvin and his childhood from Cade.

As she walked into the kitchen, she walked to the refrigerator to grab a bottle of water and jumped when she heard a sound behind her.

"Ava?"

She turned around as Cade walked in the room.

"I'm sorry. Did I wake you?" she asked. "I couldn't sleep and it's so peaceful here on the ranch. I love walking around in the evenings after I get Camico down."

"I love it here, too, which is why Callie and I had a house built on the property."

"Did I wake Callie, too? I know she needs her rest. Between all of her work on that new clothing line and looking after Colby, she is probably drained once her head hits the pillow," she quipped.

"No, she's still sleeping and nothing would wake her right now. Colby has a terrible sleeping habit as many babies do, but the past few nights, she's been sleeping better so Callie has been sleeping better. I asked her if she wanted to hire someone to help with Colby and she said no. She would rather hire extra staff at the office building. She wants Colby to only know her when it comes to her care and I respect that."

"I can, too. One day when I have children, I'm going to do the same thing. I don't want anyone else raising my children except for me."

"Things are pretty serious with and Calvin, huh?" Cade said, grabbing a bottle of water for them both.

"Yes. I love your brother with everything in me and Camico won me over the first time I held him."

"I can see that Cal loves you, too and I'm glad. I didn't know Camico's mother and in fact, I knew nothing of her until Calvin was hurt. He's never been in love that I know of before her and now with you, I see that he's head over heels in love with you. You and Camico give him purpose beyond the military and I want that for him."

"I'm glad that we can be what each other needs. He means the world to me and I'm looking forward to what's next."

"So am I. I heard you moving around and I thought I'd come check on you. I like to keep an ear and eye on what's going on around the house and I've noticed each night you seem to be up and it seems like something is bothering you. Is everything alright?" Cade asked.

"I didn't mean to make you worry. I'm fine. I'm worried about Calvin. We haven't heard from him in two weeks. How do we know he's okay?" she asked.

"I've been through this and I've been where you are with worrying about him. If he in any danger, we would hear about that before we hear he's okay. I know he wouldn't want you to worry and he couldn't do the job he has to do if he had to worry about you and Camico. You should get some sleep. Camico will be up in a few hours and though Callie and I can look after him, I think he'd prefer to have you after he checks every room and doesn't see Calvin. He sure loves his daddy."

"I love watching them together, especially when Camico is sleepy and ready for bed. He crawls up into Calvin's lap, finds that perfect spot, yarns a few times and you can see his whole body relax as if he knows he's in the safety of his father's arms. They have a perfect love," Ava said.

"That perfect love now includes you and we're happy to have you around," Cade said.

"Thanks for letting us stay here with you and Callie."

"Feel free to come here and stay anytime and not just when Calvin is mixed up in something dangerous. Besides, the security around this place is like Fort Knox. Callie's father is no joke when it comes to protecting what's his. He's got me rethinking my own security detail. I'm already putting Aaron on task to add to my team."

"You're right. I went out earlier to take Camico for a walk in his stroller and I didn't even realize one of the men was near us until a rabbit jumped out of the brush and I look up and one of his men waved at me to let me know he was all over that rabbit if need be. I'm glad Calvin put all of this in place to secure our safety while he ties up loose ends, but I can't help how worried I am about him."

"I know you are, but wearing the floor out won't help and you're going to be tired in the morning. Why don't you go try and lie down until you fall back to sleep?"

Ava knew he meant well and he was right, she would be exhausted in the morning if she didn't get some sleep.

"You're right and I am tired. I'll see you in the morning."

"Good night," Cade said.

Ava headed up the stairs and turned to see Cade check to be sure the team was still patrolling the grounds of the house. He looked out of several windows before speaking into a call box on the wall. This family was serious about security and she understood why. Cade was a mega-superstar and was always a target for those who like and did not like him all because of his star-status.

The minute she entered the room, she went first to Camico's crib to check on him and found that he was sleeping soundly.

Climbing back into bed, she snuggled deeply and hoped that Calvin was alright and prayed that he would return soon.

As sleep was just about to overtake her, Ava's cell phone rang. Reaching before it before it woke Camico, she smiled the minute she saw Calvin's name on the screen.

"Hello?" she said.

"Hi, baby."

"Calvin, you're okay?" she asked.

"I'm fine. How are you and Camico?" he asked.

"We're fine. Worried about you and missing you."

"Sounds to me like I didn't wake you up. It's three in the morning. Why do you sound like you haven't been to sleep?" he asked.

"I was worried about you. We haven't heard anything in two weeks and tonight, I couldn't seem to fall asleep."

"That's because you're not in my arms where you should be. I'd help you fall asleep. I'm the best sleep medicine there is," he said in a sexy undertone that he knew she loved.

"That's easy for you to say considering you're someplace you won't tell me about."

Calvin laughed.

"Who said I'm someplace you don't know about. Like you, I was missing you like crazy and I thought that if I'm going to get any rest myself tonight, I need to have you in my arms."

Excited flowed through her body at the thought of being in his arms, feeling his skin against hers.

"Don't tease me like that. I need you desperately right now and I've been struggling with imagining being in your arms and wanting to be in your arms."

"Well, if you come to the top of the steps, maybe, just maybe, I can do something about that," he said and then laughed.

Ava wasn't sure she heard him correctly, but just in case he was speaking the truth, she shot out of bed, yanked the bedroom door open and ran for the top of the stairs. When she was about to run down, Calvin appeared on the top step. Without thinking of anything, but the touch and feel of him, Ava leaped into his arms and cried as he kissed her all over face. While he was trying to plaster her face with kisses, she was doing the same to his face, happy that she could touch and feel him again.

"You're here!" she shouted and then covered her mouth.

"You want to wake everyone?" he laughed.

Ava hugged him even harder. She was over-excited that she could touch and feel him, knowing he made it back home in one piece.

"Are you okay? Are you hurt in any way?" she asked, feeling over him to assess any wounds or places on his body that pained him.

Calvin laughed, trying hard to stifle the sound to not wake Callie. After talking to Cade to let him know he was pulling up to the house, he mentioned the fact that Ava had just gone upstairs to bed and everyone else in the house had been sleep for hours. He knew there was no way he would be able to be anyplace other than with Ava and Camico, even if they were asleep.

"I'm okay and in a few minutes when I have you naked, I'll be perfect," he said.

"We can't do that. Camico is in the same room

I'm in," she said.

Instead of going into the room he knew Camico was always in, he turned in the opposite way and went to one of the guest bedrooms at the other end of the house.

"He'll sleep through the rest of the night. Right now, I need you," he said.

"I need you, too."

"Good and then in the morning, we're going to talk about making our love more permanent for the three of us because we're meant to be together.

When they reached the bedroom, Calvin closed the door behind them, never placing Ava down until they reached the bed. With a swiftness, he removed his clothes and laughed as he watched Ava do the same thing.

"I guess this means we're not going to talk about the past two weeks?" Ava asked.

"I'm going to say a few things and then we're going to live in the present, okay?"

"Okay."

"Valencio is no longer a threat to us, ever and I brought Sofia's body back to the United States so that my son can visit her resting place when he grows up. We're a family, I love you, you love me and we love Camico. I'm not going back to the military because I want to build a life with you and my son where I'm present. When the house if finished being remodeled, we're going to home and I hope we'll be moving into it together."

Calvin stopped talking and joined her on the bed where he pulled the covers back and slipped in next to her.

"I'm ready for where life is about to take us and I'm glad we can now live in peace."

"Me too, baby and for the rest of this night, the only talking I want to do is to let you know how good it feels to be right here with you again."

Before Ava could respond, the kissed her while at the same time covering her body with his. He kissed her hungrily, desperately, nipping and tugging on her tongue with his teeth. He missed loving her like this and thought about nothing else, besides loving her and seeing his son again.

Calvin could feel his body harden and could feel as his straining erection pushed against her softness. The minute Ava reached between them and stroked him from base to tip, he knew coming to her tonight was the perfect decision.

He moved down her body, taking one of her breasts into his mouth while he rolled the tip of the other between his fingers. The moment he felt Ava moving around under him, he knew that their need for each other had reached an epic point.

"I need you, Calvin," she whispered in his ear.

"You have me, baby. All of me," he uttered as Ava writhed around under him.

Ava spread her legs allowing more room for Calvin and as he legs went up and around his strong waste, she held her breath at the feel of his hardness entering her body which was ready for his entry. They kissed, loved and moved together, in sync with a passion that could only burn deep for each other.

Ava's arms encircled Calvin's body and caressed his muscled back that flexed as he stroked in and out of her bringing them both the pleasure they'd missed out on for the past few weeks.

Calvin bent his head and found that place on the left side of Ava's neck that he knew drove her crazy and the moment he touched her with his lips, she bucked her hips up to match his thrusts down to meet her. He could feel Ava racing for that ultimate feeling of satisfaction and he wanted that for her.

"Let yourself go, baby," he said in her ear. The moment he captured the lobe between his lips and sucked and licked on it, he felt her come apart. He was close himself and wanted to be with her. He groaned as softly as he could, remembering they were not at his house or her place, but in his brother's house even though they were several rooms away from the master suite.

"Yes!" Ava screamed softly and then Calvin let go.

He gave into the feeling, into the warmth of her body, matching her rhythm as one turbulent wave after the other crashed through him setting his body ablaze with a fierce release.

As the tremors that took them higher and higher began to subside, Calvin slowed the pace of their lovemaking, but stayed intimately connected.

"You know, if we continue to make love like this and without protection, Camico is going to end up with a little brother or sister sooner than we had planned. I want to marry you," he said, rising up to look Ava in the face. "I love you and I want you to marry me. I told you when I got back and the past would now live in the past, I wanted to make our love a permanent love. Camico and I love and need you in our lives. I don't want stolen nights with you knowing that we're not one the way we should be. I want to come home to you every day when I leave the office or when I have to take a trip away. I want Camico to have the stability of love from both of us all the time and I want to be the man you want, need and love and I want to be that man as your husband. Will you marry me?" he asked.

Ava was overwhelmed as her body surged to life again with want for the man who was her everything.

"Yes, I will marry you. I love you, too and as far as us making love like to mad lovers making Camico a big brother sooner rather than later, we're too late," she said and waited to see if Calvin would pick up on what she said. She knew the second he caught on when he stiffened above her. When their eyes locked, she knew he understood.

"You're pregnant?"

"I am, just a few weeks. You're going to be a daddy again and I hope you're ready to be a husband and a father to two young children."

Calvin shocked them both when he pumped his fist in the air and screamed.

"Yes!" he said.

Ava punched him lightly on the arm.

"You're going to wake everyone. I take it you're happy about the baby?"

"Happy? I'm super happy. I know we didn't plan on it, though our amorous activities didn't go along with preventing it, I couldn't be happier. I hope that means you're going to marry me soon?" he asked.

"I'm going to marry you as soon as you're ready and we can make it happen. My sister won't have much longer where she can travel and I want her and my brother there."

"Whatever you want is exactly what we'll do. I love you," Calvin said kissing her and letting the kiss say everything he wanted to say and more.

"I love you."

"You and Camico are why my heart beats."

EPILOGUE

Cade and Calvin rushed through the airport, with Cade's security team following close behind, to get to the plane that was set to take them to Florida for Cameron's college graduation. The rest of the family would be joining them in a few days, but they wanted to have some brother time together.

Callie was back at the house getting Colby ready and now that she was walking, she was a handful to keep up with.

Ava was overseeing the final redecorations at the house she and Calvin lived in with Camico. She was a few months away from giving birth to their first child together and settling in as wife and mother three months after they were married in a small ceremony that included her brother and sister, their families as well as Callie's family. A few months ago, their grandparents had finally moved to Texas and decided to buy Ava's condo after falling in love with it. Life was as close to perfect as one family could get.

"We're going to be late," Calvin said, checking the time.

Cade looked at him and dismissed his comment.

"We can't be late when I own the plane. We're fine and we're going a few days early to have some time with just the three of us."

"Yeah, I'm excited about that. We don't get enough time like this."

"Can you believe our baby brother is a college graduate?" Cade asked.

"I know it's crazy. I'm proud of him."

Walking through the airport private entrance to the tarmac where his plan was, Cade shook his head in agreement.

"I'm proud of both of you. I'm also glad you're staying home and that you're officially honorably discharged. I know how much the military means to you, but family is just as important. With the new baby coming, you're needed with your wife and children."

"Can you believe I'm about to be a father again? There was a time I didn't see myself having kids at all and now I'm about to have my second. I couldn't be happier."

Finally at the plane, they entered and Cade gave the pilot instructions to take off as soon as possible. While they waited for the pre-flight check to be completed, Cade's cell phone rang.

"Cam? What's going on?" he asked.

"Nothing. I'm checking to make sure you and Cal

are still coming down to Florida early."

"We're on our way. Everything okay?"

"Oh, yeah. Everything is good. I want to talk to you about my graduate studies."

"Are you still pursuing a degree in Journalism?" Cade asked.

"I am. My coach is surprised I'm not playing professional ball. All the talk is about me being a first round pick in the draft, but that's not where my heart is," Cameron said.

"Why do I hear reservation in your voice?"

"I don't know. I'm wondering if I'm making a mistake not going pro. That could mean big things for me."

Cade laughed.

"Right, you mean it would raise your status with the women if you were a pro-athlete."

He heard Cameron chuckle on the other end.

"Yeah, that, too. Come on, you were all about the ladies before you found the perfect woman and settled down and so did Calvin. Now, you're both married and all in love. I'm too young for that and I could really break a few hearts hear and there if my status was professional athlete. You know how the women love ball players. I'm trying to pick up with the ladies where you left off," he quipped.

"You don't have to be a ball player to be a heartbreaker. You're a Lymon and therefore, being a heartbreaker comes naturally. Don't talk down on a career as an on-air television personality. You'll be on every screen across the country and the women will still lust after you. Be careful, bro. You may find yourself all happy and in love like Cal and me. Don't knock it until you try it," Cade jested.

"Nah, bro. I'm always going to be a heartbreaker. I'm not the falling in love type," he said.

Laughing out loud, Cade had a hard time getting himself together. His little brother had no clue. When love strikes, he'll be immune to fight it, too.

"There you go uttering those famous last words."

"Trust me, Cade. I'll be a heartbreaking playboy forever!"

**Coming up next from *A Lovers' Heart*
book series, *Heartbreaker*,
Cameron Lymon's story.**

Cameron Lymon is fresh out of college with his Master's degree in Journalism with a minor in Communications and Sports Management and has landed a job that has never been offered to someone fresh out of school. Heading off to Denver, Colorado to start his career as the co-anchor for a new morning show, he isn't prepared for the steamy encounters with his co-host ten years older than him and fifty shades hot. What started as casual hookups, soon leads to more than just clandestine rendezvous around the station. Cameron was losing his heart and his playboy status for a woman who showed him how to stop playing at love and just love.

Cameron's story is coming to you in late 2018.

Coming up in August 2018,
***Behind Closed Doors*, a new spicy,**
romantic release.

Princess Yasmine had an image to uphold as the daughter of the King of a country. She was pledged in marriage by her father in order to build her family's wealth, but a few last flings wouldn't hurt anybody, or so she thought.

Kennard Jackson is a music mogul and playboy and is known for satisfying the ladies. For the first time in his life, he found a woman who was beyond his reach until she made the first move and then all bets were off.

Get Books One – Four of the *Bachelor Series*

Book One - *Bachelor Not for Sale* – Now available

Even self-proclaimed "bachelors for life" meet that one woman that makes them want to slow down and second guess bachelorhood. After suffering through the heartache of what he thought was true love, Duron Knight meets and becomes enchanted with bombshell Taija Charles.

Taija has heard a lot about Duron and all of her

body senses are on overdrive when she meets the handsome bachelor face to face. As the sparks fly, Taija plans to show Duron how she can help him mend his broken heart with real love and the right amount of lust.

Book Two – *A Designed Affair* – Now available

In the follow-up to "Bachelor Not for Sale", Loren Knight has been engaging in a secret love affair with her brother Duron's best friend and business partner, Michael Bailey. He is everything she could want and more in a man, but she believes the risk is too great for any type of relationship with him beyond the bedroom door.

Michael Bailey has been fighting his attraction to Loren for years. He has stayed away from her out of respect for his best friend and business partner. Now that he and Loren have finally given into passion that they both have been craving, can Michael convince Loren that what they share is worth the risk?

Book Three – *A Perfect Combination* – Now available

In the third installment following "Bachelor Not for Sale" and "A Designed Affair", Tyrone Davis is the king of one-night stands; nicknamed, Mr. Love

Them and Leave Them. He learned to perfect it from his two best friends, Duron Knight and Michael Bailey. He never imagined a one-night stand would have such a lasting impact, but that's exactly what happened.

Victoria Alston couldn't forget the incredible night she spent with Tyrone Davis, someone connected to one of her best friends. The next day, she disappeared, returning to reality and the fiancé she'd left in Boston while on business travel. They both soon discovered that it wasn't just a one-night stand, but a perfect combination for love.

Book Four – *Love at Last* – Now available

They had the perfect love...That's what Brian Knight thought of his relationship with Sherry Braxton until he looked up one day and she was gone and never wanted to see him again.

Two years later, he discovered that there is the possibility that Sherry may have been pregnant with his child. Hurt and angry at her deceit, he takes a flight to Baltimore to fight for his rights as a father and realizes that the love and passion they once shared had never died.

Is it possible he could still have the kind of love he

thought would last a lifetime? Can he still have his love at last?

From Cheryl Barton – *Un-Break My Heart* – Now Available

Dr. Mackenzie Ellis suffered a loss so great, she never thought she'd fall in love again, especially with someone close to her.

Travis Blackwell, III never dreamed of crossing the line with Mackenzie until his heart would no longer allow him to deny the love he has for her and the passion he wants to share with her knowing that he is the key to mending her broken heart.

From Cheryl Barton – *Bossy* – Now Available

Cassidy 'Bossy' Bostic came from nothing, but knew she would be something. Pregnant and alone, she was forced to run from her past in order to have a future. Her rise to the top as the owner of a fashion dynasty is what dreams are made of, but her hard, icy persona could have her living a lonely existence.

Drake Montgomery, a rising attorney heading toward the political arena, has fallen in love with the 'Bossy' mogul only to discover it's 'Cassidy' he loves, but 'Bossy', not so much.

Can their hot, steamy romance melt even her cold, icy heart? Only time and love will tell.

From Cheryl Barton – *Heartthrob* – Now Available

Cade Weston, Hollywood's most eligible bachelor and named the world's sexiest man of the year, lives life at the top with a bevy of beauties at his beck and call, people providing his every desire and more money than any one person should have.

Callie Hurston struggles to make it as a stylist to the stars in a world where women are intimidated by her beauty and men are interested in her body and not her talent.

Cade thought he had it all until he has a chance meeting with Callie and decides to take a chance on her talent and ends up taking an even bigger chance with his heart.

Can the playboy turn in his player's card and give in to love?

From Cheryl Barton – *His Halloween Promise* – Now Available

Dylan Kennedy and Savannah Eaton-Kennedy may be divorced, but that doesn't stop them from indulging in some pretty hot and sexy encounters.

A divorce decree may mean that their life together is over, but Dylan has a promise to keep that could bring his wife back where she belongs; in his life permanently.

From Cheryl Barton – *Home for Thanksgiving* – Now Available

Firefighter Nicholas Sullivan is going home for the holiday after he was sidelined due to an injury on the job. Guilt over a life lost has kept him away from his family's ranch in Montana and now he's forced to face his past demons and deal with a self-imposed life of regret.

Veterinarian Parker Wingate's first encounter with the handsome firefighter was less than pleasurable. She sympathized with his hurt, understood his pain and before long, felt his love.

Knowing the holiday season is ending soon, can Nick go from living in love for the moment to allowing himself to finally live in love forever?

From Cheryl Barton – *A Better Man* – Now Available

Phoenix Graham is living her best life with the best man, her fiancé, Carson Stone, heir to the Stone Tower Hotel Empire. Her perfect life is shaken up when a handsome, rugged and extremely sexy mysterious man moves in across the hall and she begins to see that the rose-colored glasses she had been seeing life through were blinders. She soon discovers that Carson was the best man for her until she takes notice of a better man and his name is Gavin Black.

What's a girl to do when the best doesn't get better and better is what she craves?

From Cheryl Barton
Book Five of the *Amorous Occupations* series, *The Electrician* – Now Available

The party invitation said everyone had to wear a masquerade mask the entire night, a New Orleans tradition. Dara Marshall couldn't resist the opportunity to spend an uninhibited night of passion with National Football Association coach Nelson Riley, the guest of honor, knowing that her identity was hidden by her mask.

Dara's world turns upside down when she discovers the gorgeous coach is the newest client of her father's business and after she's sent on a job at his condo, she does everything in her power to not give away the secret of who she is.

Nelson could never forget the sexy temptress he'd spent an unforgettable night with, even when she tries to hide behind a mask and baggy overalls.

All books are available on my website at
www.cherylbarton.net

To my friends who love reading and experiencing love, I want to thank you for your support and your friendship!

I am because you read - Cheryl

Connect with me

Visit my website at www.CherylBarton.net
Twitter – @Author Cheryl Barton
Instagram – AuthorCherylBarton
Facebook at Author Cheryl Barton
Email – Cheryl@CherylBarton.net
Blog - https://mswriterinmd.wordpress.com/

About the Author

Cheryl Barton lives in Maryland and in her spare time she loves to read espionage novels, cook, watch Sci-fi movies, spend time with family and friends and enjoy Maryland steamed crabs.

Indulge in more romance and inspirational novels by visiting her website at www.cherylbarton.net.

Cheryl is a member of the Romance Writers of America – National Chapter and the Maryland Romance Writers.